Diane E. Lindmark

Life takes you different directions

Diane E. Lindmark

Text copyright © 2017 Diane E. Lindmark

All Rights Reserved

This book or any portion thereof may not be reproduced or used in any manner whatsoever without the express written permission of the publisher except for the use of brief quotations in a book review.

All characters appearing in this work are fictitious. Any resemblance to real persons, living or dead, is purely coincidental.

2023-06

If you enjoyed this book please check out these other books by Diane E. Lindmark

The Stone Family Series

A Solitary Stone Book 1 of the Stone Wall Trilogy
A Stone Falls Book 2 of the Stone Wall Trilogy
The Stone Wall Book 3 of the Stone Wall Trilogy
Heart of Stone Part 1 Passage of Stone
Heart of Stone Part 2 A Stone Divided
The Measure of a Man
Lady Huntsman
Founding Fathers
Hidden Stories

The McLoughlin Family

Safe Haven
Any Port in a Storm
The Eye of the Storm
Storm Bringer
Corruption or Luck

The Crosses

The Christmas Hitchhiker
The Christmas Breakdown
The Christmas Derailment
The Christmas Avalanche
The Christmas Reboot
Dukes and Plumbers
Bjorn in America

Demented Fairy Tales

A Castle Frozen in Time

One Off's

Second Age of Darkness
The Kith
Land and Treachery
One Man's Wife
Legacy
An Accident of Faith
The Wrong Life
For Family Honor
Rough Road

I

Grand Central Station, New York City
Wednesday, June 27, 1906

Claudette could barely contain her excitement. She was finally getting to go home. She had not been home in four years. Her parents and siblings had been able to come and visit her twice; but given the length of the journey it was not an easy thing to do, and her short breaks did not permit her to go home and visit them. She had never regretted anything as much as she had regretted begging her parents to send her to New York to go to school. She wished she would have just begged her parents to take her to New York for a visit, or maybe send her for a summer to visit her aunt and uncle. She had wanted so desperately to see where her mother had grown up, but she had been here a little more than a month when she had seen everything she wanted to see. Most important of these was the Statue of Liberty, which her mother had heard about, but not seen in its entirety. Though she had seen the arm bearing the torch when it was on display in Madison Square Park in Manhattan; her mother's first husband, Mr. O'Brien, had taken her to see it. They even been photographed with it. She had walked the Brooklyn Bridge, something her mother had done many a time, though her mother had not gotten to see the site of the Statue of Liberty from it. Of course, one could not resist having lunch in the Waldorf and the Astoria, though both these buildings were not built until after mother had left, but once her sightseeing was over, she found how desperately she missed home. She could have easily written her parents and told them she had made a mistake and she wanted to come home. They would have gladly brought her home, but she had asked for this, and she had committed herself to four years of school. She had to finish what she had started, that was only the right thing to do, but she was never going to leave Texas again, she missed it too much. She missed all of her aunts and uncles. She even missed her younger siblings. The only good thing to come out of her four years in New York was it gave her an opportunity to get to know her Uncle Sean and Aunt Suzanne. She got to spend all of her holidays with them, so it was almost like being home, but not quite. She missed her own family. Her thoughts were interrupted by Uncle Sean approaching.

He offered her several pieces of paper. "Here are your tickets and your baggage claim checks. As you requested, you're routed through Chicago and then on home to Donegal."

She took them and placed them in her reticule, then hugged him tightly. "Thank you so much for everything, Uncle Sean." She turned and embraced her aunt. "Thank you for letting me spend so much time with your family."

Suzanne embraced her. "You are most welcome, my darling. We greatly enjoyed the opportunity to get to know you. You are welcome any time."

Sean produced his pocket watch and looked at the time. He said with only mild annoyance, "Where is that escort the school is supposed to be sending?" He looked around and then added, "I really think I should've engaged your escort."

Claudette patted him on the arm. "Don't worry, Uncle. I'm sure if the school employed him, he has impeccable references and the appropriate skills."

Sean was not sure of this at all. A moment later, a middle-aged man approached. Sean looked him up and down and hoped desperately that this was not to be Claudette's escort. The man tipped his hat. "Good morning, ladies, sir. Perchance might you be Miss Claudette McLoughlin?"

"I am Claudette McLoughlin, and you are …?"

He removed his hat, produced a card, and offered it to her. She took it. "Mark Walker. I am employed by Colfax University. I was sent to escort you home, Miss McLoughlin." The elderly gentleman held out his hand. Mark hesitated a moment, then produced another card and handed it to him.

Sean took the card and read it. 'Mark Walker, University security office, Colfax University'. Sean shook his head firmly. "Claudette, I am not comfortable with this at all, and I do not think your father would approve. I think it is best if you wait and travel another day when I can employ ... a more suitable escort."

Claudette's eyes widened and she shook her head. "Oh no, please, Uncle Sean, that could take days! I'm sure that he has done this many times." She looked at Mr. Walker hopefully.

Mark cleared his throat and said, trying not to sound offended, "I have been employed by the University for fifteen years, and in that time I have been asked more than fifty times to escort young ladies of good family home. Though I will say this is the first time I've ever been required to travel as far as Texas, I am quite sure I can manage a simple train journey."

Sean looked the man up and down again. Forty, tall, slightly built with spectacles, not the kind of man he would wish as an escort for his niece. He opened his mouth with every intention of saying 'Absolutely not!', but he felt someone squeeze his arm. He looked down.

Suzanne said gently, "Sean, my love, I am sure that there will be no problems. All he is doing is making sure that Claudette makes it home. There's not going to be any trouble."

"Yes, Uncle Sean, for heaven sakes, this is nineteen o six."

The conductor began calling, "All aboard!"

Sean growled and nodded grudgingly. "Against my better judgment, I will permit it, but you had better see that nothing happens to my niece. The last enemy you want on this earth is O'Brien Shipping, do I make myself clear?"

Claudette and Suzanne looked at each other and rolled their eyes. They all embraced one more time, then she and Mr. Walker boarded the train.

II

Oklahoma
Saturday, June 30, 1906

Fifty miles! Only fifty miles and she would be back in Texas! She looked out the window. It was just a little before dawn. She guessed they would be arriving in Donegal around four this afternoon. She could not wait. She got up and got dressed, then permitted the porter to set her compartment to rights while she went and had her breakfast. She was just finishing her breakfast when Mr. Walker arrived. She preferred to think of him as her chaperone rather than her bodyguard. When she had traveled to New York, Uncle Leopold had escorted her. That had been much more enjoyable and felt safer. She knew Uncle Leopold would let nothing happen to her. Unfortunately, Mr. Walker was not her idea of a bodyguard. He did not carry a gun, and she was fairly certain he did not even know how to fight, and she doubted seriously his presence would scare anyone away. After all, he was what was referred to as a dude, at least in Texas. She smiled as she gently patted her hip. Her traveling gown had a concealed pocket where she had placed the nice little two shot derringer her father had given her before she had left home. Any time she had gone anywhere, it had been her companion. She decided it was better not to tell Uncle Sean. After all, he was a city man. He might not approve of his niece carrying a gun. She had only ever had to use it once when a thug stepped out of an alley with a knife and tried to grab her reticule. Fortunately, knowing she was not in the most reputable part of town, she had already had her hand in her pocket, ready for anything. The thug had stared at her for a moment, then turned and fled. She had put it back in her pocket and hurried on her way. She, unlike Mr. Walker, was not afraid of the idea of shooting someone, but she guessed that was the difference between ranch people and city people. She had been twelve when she had gotten her first rifle for Christmas. That was the thing she had missed most about living in the city, she could not wake up on Saturday morning, grab her rifle, throw some bread and an apple in her saddle bag, and go for a long ride. She looked out the window and sighed.

Mark looked up from his breakfast. "Is there something the matter, Miss McLoughlin?"

She looked back at him, hesitated a moment, and then said, "I was just wondering what the likelihood that this is the same train my mother had traveled on when she came from New York."

Mark refrained from rolling his eyes. He found Miss McLoughlin to be a bit silly. She had some of the most fanciful ideas. He still rather resented the fact that their train journey was a day longer because she had purchased the tickets taking them through Chicago, a wholly unnecessary extension of their trip. Had she had business in Chicago, that would have been different, but she wanted to travel home on the exact rail lines her mother had traveled to Texas twenty years earlier. He tried not to sound annoyed when he said, "I find that highly improbable."

Claudette sighed with frustration and refrained from commenting that of course he would, she found he had no imagination. She focused her attention on her empty teacup. All that was in it now was the slice of lemon. She contemplated pouring more, but then decided against it. As she contemplated it a moment, approaching footsteps caught her attention. She looked up to see the waiter approaching. She asked hopefully, "Do you know if we have crossed into Texas yet?"

The elderly gentleman leaned down a little to look out the window, then he nodded. "Yes, ma'am, I believe we have, but only barely."

She gave him a dazzling smile. "Thank you so much." She turned back to Mr. Walker. "Almost home." To her annoyance, he did not look impressed. She sighed again, got to her feet, and headed back to her private compartment.

When Mr. Walker joined her, she looked out the window and ignored his presence. He produced a book and began reading. She watched the countryside go by. They had been sitting in cool silence for at least an hour when all of a sudden the train came to a screeching halt. Claudette, who was sitting with her back to the engine, was thrown to the floor. A moment later, her ears perked up. She was sure she had just heard gunshots. She hesitated only a moment, then she got to her feet and grabbed Mr. Walker, who looked confused. "It would be a bad idea for us to be in a private compartment when they find us. We should go and sit in one of the passenger cars."

Mark stared at the foolish girl for a moment. "Miss McLoughlin, I really think that it is better for us to stay where we are."

She shook her head. "If you desire to stay here, you stay here. I would rather be around people, thank you." She exited her compartment. Several passengers were in the aisle looking confused. She headed for one of the passenger cars. She was just opening the door from the sleeper, about to cross to the passenger car, when a man with a bandanna tied around his face opened the passenger door. The two of them locked eyes.

He laughed and said, "Lookee, lookee what we got here! Weren't thinking about getting away, were you?" He looked down and snatched her reticule off her wrist.

She grabbed her wrist. "Ow, that hurt and was completely unnecessary! I would've given it to you had you asked."

Mark gripped her by the shoulders, trying to pull her back as he said, "Claudette, it is not wise to speak that way to an armed man."

The outlaw looked her up and down. He reached out with his free hand and touched her cheek. "Yeah, Claudette, you should show your betters respect."

She decided it was more tactful not to comment on that. Instead she said politely, "Aren't you in the middle of a train robbery? Shouldn't you get back to it?"

The outlaw backhanded her so hard she hit the exterior wall of the train and slid down. "I'd watch that smart mouth of yours, little miss. It's gonna get you in a lot of trouble."

Mark jumped back and stared momentarily in horror, then he said haughtily, "Now see here, that was completely unnecessary!"

Kenny stepped forward and decked the dude in front of him. The dude hit the floor and did not get up. He reached down and grabbed Claudette by the arm, yanking her to her feet, then he waved his gun at the rest of the passengers. "You all move forward!" Still holding her by the arm, he stepped into one of the open compartments and watched the rest of them walk by. None of them were carrying guns and gave him no pause. Once the last of them had gone past, he pulled Claudette along as he searched the four private compartments, making sure no one was hiding. Then he followed the others. Someone apparently had helped the dude up. When they entered the passenger car, he saw the dude sitting in a seat with a handkerchief to his bleeding lip. Kenny waved his gun in the dude's direction as he demanded, "Claudette is an awful uppity name. How'd you end up traveling with that little weasel? You ain't his mistress, are you?"

Claudette tried to pull free, but he was not letting her go. She replied with irritation, "Claudette is not uppity, it's French, and how dare you! He is a friend of my Uncle's and is accompanying me home after a visit to my relatives in New York."

"Really, French? And what's your last name?"

Claudette said the first name that came to her mind. "Blanc."

"Must have some rich folks if they sent you all the way to New York just for a visit."

She tried again to jerk her arm free, saying with irritation, "Not that it's any of your business, but my grandmother was ill and my father sent me up two years ago to be of use to my uncle and aunt. It wasn't exactly a short visit. Now will you please give me back my arm?" She hoped she would not be required to remember her lies, but she had a good memory. She was sure she could if she had to, but at least if any of them spoke French, they would not find Blanc an out of the way last name. After all, it was French for white.

Two armed men entered from the other side of the car. One of them demanded, "Have you finished searching this lot?"

"No, I ain't. I ran into a bit of trouble and this uppity wench won't shut 'er damn mouth."

Claudette wanted to step on his foot for calling her a wench, but she decided it was best to remain silent. The two new arrivals began stripping the passengers of their valuables. They were about halfway to her when one of the men decided he was not going to part with his valuables. When he opened his valise, he pulled out a small derringer and shot the boy who was standing in front of him. Well, at least from his size and voice Claudette thought he was a boy, he sounded only sixteen or so. She gave a little scream and started forward. Everything happened so fast. Before she had a chance to look away, the passenger was shot in the head at point blank range with a Colt forty-five. She was certain that image was forever branded in her brain. She shut her eyes and gave a shudder, then jerked her arm again. The boy was now lying in the aisle, groaning and crying in pain. "Let me go! Maybe I can help him!" She jerked harder.

Both outlaws were yelling over each other. It was hard to tell who was saying what. One of them said, "Don't nobody else try to be stupid. Sit down and hand over your valuables."

"Anybody else want to die today, go ahead and try to be a hero." They were both waving their guns back and forth, looking for anyone to shoot.

She finally managed to jerk free and moved to the boy's side. She dropped down on her knees and applied pressure to the wound. She struggled to get him onto his side. She sighed with relief. It appeared to her that the bullet passed clean through. She tentatively probed the wound, surprised that no one else had been hit.

The boy screamed and the second outlaw demanded, "What the hell do you think you're doing?"

"I should think, you ignorant savage, the answer to that should be obvious. I'm trying to save his life, not that either one of you deserve it."

"Call me an ignorant savage again, little girl, and I'll give you a bruise to match the one you already got!"

The boy demanded, "Is it bad?"

"I know very little about these things, but it looks to have gone straight through. I don't think it hit anything vital, but you are bleeding a lot. We need to stop the bleeding." She looked up and asked, "Can I have a couple of handkerchiefs and something to hold them around the wound?"

One of her fellow passengers crossed his arms over his chest and said with irritation, "Let him bleed to death, he ain't nothing but a bandit."

She snapped with irritation, "He's barely more than a child and I wouldn't let a wounded dog suffer, let alone a human being."

The second outlaw pointed his gun at the man. "Give her your handkerchief, and while you're at it, your shirt."

The man grumbled but did as he was ordered. Several more handkerchiefs were freely offered. She applied the handkerchiefs to either side of the wound, rolled the shirt up so it made one long bandage, then using the sleeves, she wrapped it around his waist twice and pulled it tight, trying to ignore his screams and cries of protest, and tied it off. While she did this, the second outlaw watched her and the rest of her fellow passengers, and the first one finished robbing all of the passengers. Another man entered the car and demanded, "What the hell is taking so long?"

The second outlaw snapped, "Someone shot my brother! Looks like the girl's finished with him. You two get my brother, I'll cover you."

The other two outlaws did as they were told. The second outlaw grabbed her arm and said, as he began dragging her towards the door, "You're coming with us, missy."

"No! Why?"

"Because you made yourself indispensable. You like that word, indispensable? Not bad for an ignorant savage." He waved his gun back and forth at the other passengers. "Anyone gets off this train before we're out of sight and you'll be buried right alongside that one there." He gestured to the body lying backwards over one of the seats.

Claudette involuntarily looked and then shuddered. Once she was off the train, he dragged her quickly toward some horses. One of the outlaws, she was not sure which, she was losing track of who was first, second, third, fourth, fifth. She groaned, *Oh, yes, and of course there's a sixth.* Six to one ... she did not like those odds, especially not with only two bullets in her little derringer.

Jake demanded, "What the hell you bringin' her 'long for?"

Frank glared at Jake and shoved the girl in his direction. "I need her to help look after my brother! Put her on your horse and let's get out here, or do you want to stick around and wait for the Sheriff and his deputies?"

Jake wanted to argue with Frank, but he decided this was not the right moment. He took the girl by the arm and pulled her in the direction of his horse, then he grabbed her around the waist and seated her on it. He had expected her to fight and protest, or at least cry, but to his surprise, she was very silent and looked very pale. He mounted up behind her and they all lit out of there. After a minute, Kenny said with a laugh, "I think you should have put the pretty one on my horse. She doesn't seem to like Jake. She's gone green all of a sudden."

Frank shook his finger at Kenny. "Keep your damn hands off her, Kenny! Right now I need her, and that's exactly why I put her with Jake. He ain't gonna get too friendly and piss her off."

Claudette was suddenly finding it hard to breathe and despite the warm summer day, she was shaking like a leaf.

When they were out of sight of the train, Jake pulled his bandanna down and demanded, "You gonna be okay? You don't look good."

"Oh, yes, I'm going to be delightful ... I've just been kidnapped, I'm covered in blood, and I watched some ..." She shuddered and started crying, "Someone get their head blown off ... I'm just peachy." She knew she had sounded hysterical, but she just could not seem to stop herself. She wanted to bury her face in her hands and have a good cry, but the blood prevented her from doing this.

Jake shifted the reins into his left hand as he tightened his grip around her waist with it, then he reached back with his right and fiddled with his saddle bag. Finding the bottle of whiskey, he yanked it out, pulled the cork out with his teeth, and pressed it into her hand. "I think you better take a couple good swigs of this."

"No thank you, I don't drink."

He growled and shifted her in his arms, then he pressed the bottle to her lips and tilted it up. She tried to pull away, but he was preventing her. After a minute she found it impossible to catch her breath through her nose, and she involuntarily opened her mouth and sucked in some of the whiskey. He pulled the bottle away and let her catch her breath, then he forced it to her mouth again. When Jake felt she taken in at least a shot, he put the cork back in the bottle and stuffed it back in his saddle bag. She was coughing and sputtering. "Now you'll feel more yourself in a few minutes."

She grabbed her throat and said hoarsely, "I find that impossible to believe." To her great annoyance, after a few minutes, the shivering stopped, and she did feel a little more like herself. She wished he did not notice, but he did, and she found she had the overwhelming urge to slap that smug look off his face, but since he could easily throw her to the ground and trample her, she decided that was probably a bad idea and gave a little huff and looked forward, therefore avoiding looking at him.

III

Caleb McLoughlin paced up and down the train platform. The train was now an hour late. He glanced at Dani sitting, waiting patiently. He smiled. She never ceased to take his breath away. He stood there a moment longer admiring his wife, then someone calling his name caught his attention. He looked to see Mary Patterson standing in front of the post office waving at him. She yelled, "Caleb, there's a man on the telephone for you."

Caleb and Dani exchanged worried looks. He offered his hand to her, she took it, and he assisted her to her feet. They hurried to the post office. Caleb hesitated only a moment before putting the telephone to his ear. He had only used the thing a half dozen times in his life, he still found it quite peculiar. He said a little uncertainly, "This is Caleb McLoughlin, who am I speaking to?"

A voice from faraway said, "Mr. McLoughlin, you don't know me. My name is Mark Walker, I'm a member of Colfax University security, and I was assigned to escort your daughter, Miss McLoughlin, home. We were approximately fifty miles on this side of the Texas border when the train was attacked by robbers. There was some shooting and one of the passengers was killed. I don't know how to tell you this." Walker hesitated.

Caleb snapped angrily, "Did they hurt my daughter? Is she all right?"

"One of the men slapped her across the face, but they've taken her."

Caleb swallowed hard. He felt his heart drop into his stomach. He gripped the edge of the counter. Dani grabbed ahold of his arm with both hands. He reached out and wrapped his arm around her waist and pulled her against him, his hand pressed into her back. "Where are you?"

"I am in Pampa, but the train was robbed somewhere between Pampa and Miami, Texas, but what I wanted to know is what do you wanted me to do. Your daughter told everyone her name was Claudette Blanc ... do you want me to correct it ..."

Caleb cut him off quickly. "No! Whatever you do, don't correct it! The last thing we want is it in all the papers that she's been kidnapped. Why did they take her?"

"One of the robbers had been shot. She looked after his wounds ..." The line went dead.

Caleb grumbled and swore under his breath. He shook the stupid thing and asked "Mary, can you get him back?"

She took the receiver and tried for several minutes. Caleb took this opportunity to relay the whole conversation to Dani. Finally, Mary said, "I'm so sorry, Caleb, but it's down on their end and I can't get through."

Dani was struggling to think. After a long minute she asked, "You want to go after them, don't you?"

"They took my daughter! Of course I do! But as much as I hate to admit it, I ain't as young as I used to be. I want to, I want to real bad!"

Dani reached up and squeezed his arm. "I think we should call Matt Crawford. I'm sure he still works for the Pinkertons."

Caleb grumbled, but nodded and tapped the stupid telephone. "Can you get Dallas on this stupid thing? Do you think you can get the Pinkertons?"

Mary shrugged her shoulders. "I can see if the lines are up between here and there. If not, we can telegraph."

Dani said quickly, "Telegraph first, then we'll try calling him."

Caleb picked up one of the telegraph forms, but found he just could not focus on written words. He handed it over to Dani. She hesitated a moment and began writing. When she was finished, she handed it to Caleb. He took it and read it. 'To Dallas Texas from Donegal Texas. Care of Pinkerton's National Detective Agency attention Matt Crawford. Train robbery outside Pampa Texas. Daughter kidnapped by outlaws. Want to hire you and as many men as you need to get her back. Discretion and tact essential. I hope you remember us and our mutual friend Fielder. Caleb and Dani.' He nodded with approval. "If that doesn't jog his memory, he don't deserve to call himself a Pinkerton." He handed it over to Mary, saying, "Send that."

Then he turned and hugged Dani tightly, saying with more confidence than he felt, "She's our daughter. She's tough, she'll be all right."

Dani smiled. "Don't you mean she's your daughter? She's tough, she knows how to take care of herself, because you saw to that."

He tilted her chin up. "We saw to that."

IV

Claudette found it incredibly uncomfortable riding sidesaddle. She was certain they had been on horseback for more than an hour when they arrived at a nondescript looking little shack. It had a small stable next to it, a horse trough, and a well. There was a large pond about a hundred paces from the shack. Jake dismounted and pulled her off the saddle. He held her for a moment while feeling returned to her legs. She wanted to shove him away, but she knew if she did she would collapse. She gripped his forearms to steady herself. After a moment, she felt as though she could stand on her own. She pulled free and stood there feeling dazed.

"You there, girlie, come look at my brother," snapped the second outlaw.

She nodded grudgingly and moved towards the boy. As she knelt down, she could smell the whiskey. "How much alcohol have you given him?"

"As much as he needed to help with the pain," snapped the man.

She glared up at him. "And what am I supposed to call you, and for that matter, what is his name, or should I just continue to call you outlaw number two and outlaw number three?"

Jake snickered.

"I'm Frank Ramirez, and this is my brother José."

"Well, Mr. Ramirez, it's not advisable for you to give him anymore liquor. As I understand it, it thins the blood and makes clotting more difficult." She began pulling the bandages back and sighed. "He's still bleeding. We're going to have to stitch him up." She turned to Kenny and demanded, "You do still have my reticule, don't you?"

He began digging around in the bag. "This one yours?"

She looked over her shoulder. "Yes. There should be a spool of button thread and a needle. Bring them to me, and do you have any of that whiskey left, or did you pour it all in him? And somebody get some water on to boil."

Frank said, "Sam, get a bottle for the girl! Walt, put some water on to boil! Anything else Your Highness needs?"

She turned and glared at him. "Yes, Mr. Ramirez, a bar of soap, if you have such a thing. It would also do you well to remember I'm trying to save your brother's life." Kenny offered her the button thread. "Thank you. You wouldn't happen to have any clean cloths we can use for bandages and a blanket we can lay him on?"

Jake dropped down next to her and offered her a bar of soap. "Shouldn't we take him inside?"

"We could, but the light is better out here. I suggest we take care of him out here and then move him inside after we're done."

Jake nodded. "That makes sense, but do you actually know what you're doing?"

"Somewhat. I helped Dr. Cahill on several occasions tend to some of the wounded hands and I helped him patch up my father's shoulder after he was shot by cattle rustlers. Dr. Cahill strongly encouraged me on several occasions to go into nursing, but I didn't think then, and I definitely don't think so now, that I want to spend the rest of my life elbow deep in blood. I don't mind stepping in and helping when need be, but that's not how I want to spend my life."

She got to her feet and crossed to the well. "I need someone to pull up a bucket of water and get me another bucket I could wash my hands and arms in." Frank did as she asked. When she was finished washing her hands, she asked, "Can you get me another bucket of water, only half-full this time."

She returned to José's side. When she had everything she required, she stripped him to the waist, removed the bandages, and cleaned the wound. Frank and Jake ended up having to hold him down. She forced herself to focus on what she was doing, trying not to listen to his screaming, though she preferred the screaming to the crying. When she was finally finished, she cleaned all the blood off of him and bandaged the wound. Two of the men carried him inside. She wondered if José died, if Frank was going to kill her. She had done her best, but he had lost a lot of blood. He was so young, she hoped he would turn his life around and find something useful to do with the rest of his life. She hoped he would have that chance. She scrubbed her hands and then began trying to clean the blood off of her dress, she was covered in it. After a minute, she became aware that someone was watching her. She looked up to see Frank standing there, his arms crossed, studying her. She took this opportunity to actually look at him. So far, their faces were all like blurs. He was a Mexican, about twenty-five or thirty she guessed, his hair was short cropped and he had a full mustache. She studied him a moment longer. She found it interesting, though he had killed that man without hesitation, he did not appear to be cruel or evil. Not nice, definitely, but not what she would have expected. They stared at each other a moment longer, then he nodded, turned, and went to the stables. She shrugged her shoulders and went back to trying to clean herself up. He rode out a few minutes later on a fresh horse. She looked around hopefully. Her hopes were immediately dashed. Kenny and Jake were watching her at a discreet distance. She sighed and went back to trying to clean herself up. She watched them discreetly and found it interesting that Kenny was watching her intently, but Jake was dividing his attention between her and Kenny. She took this opportunity to discreetly observe both of them. Kenny was what her mother would have called a born troublemaker, the kind of man you look at and know instantly he was going to cause problems. He was not quite twenty, short, broadly built with short brown hair and brown eyes, surprisingly good looking if you went for born troublemakers. She did not. He made her skin crawl. She shifted her attention to Jake. Tall, slim, with shaggy blond hair and bright blue eyes, about twenty-five or so, with a close cropped beard and was also quite good looking, though from his attitude and demeanor, he did not seem to belong. Frank was hostile in the extreme, Kenny was a troublemaker, Jake was an enigma. She sighed. She had done everything she could do to try to improve her appearance, unfortunately, her dress was still covered in blood. In fact, she was not sure it did not look worse than before she had started, but the sun was starting to get to her. She pushed herself to her feet and headed for the shack.

The two men entered behind her. Walt demanded, "Where'd Frank go?"

Kenny replied, "He went to get some more whiskey and some more food since we got an extra mouth to feed."

Claudette looked around. By her standards, the place was filthy, but in their defense, she had seen much worse. Feeling nervous and seeing nothing else to do, she began cleaning up. To her surprise, Jake and Walt both pitched in and were perfectly happy to fetch and carry water, or anything she required.

When Frank returned three hours later, he looked around and let out a whistle. "Place looks so nice I'm starting to feel like I'm in the wrong place. Maybe we should keep a girl around more often." He walked up to her and handed her a paper wrapped parcel. "I'm sure it ain't the right size, but it's at least cleaner than what you got on. You can go take a bath in the pond."

Claudette stared at him incredulously. "Do you really think I'm going to bathe around you?"

Frank shrugged. "Suit yourself, I ain't the one with blood all over my face and neck, and it looks like you got some behind your ear and in your hair."

She gave a little gasp and touched the side of her neck. She could feel the dried blood. She gently patted her hair. She could feel it in her hair too. She must have absentmindedly touched her hair when her hands were covered in blood. She opened and closed her mouth several times, being unsure of what to say.

Frank laughed. "If you're worried about Kenny being a Peeping Tom, you can stop. I'll keep him inside and let Jake keep an eye on you to make sure you don't run off."

Jake demanded with irritation, "Why do I keep getting stuck babysitting?"

Frank laughed and replied, "Because I can trust you keep your hands to yourself. I don't trust myself that much and I sure as hell don't trust Kenny or Walt. And Sam, well, he'd probably let her wander off, and José is in no condition, so that just leaves you."

Jake growled and got to his feet. "So just how long are you planning on keeping her around?"

"As long as José needs her around. When he doesn't need her anymore, we'll re-evaluate the situation."

Jake growled again, grabbed her by the arm, and dragged her out the door. As he walked past the bucket she had washed her hands in, he picked up the soap. Arriving at the pond, he snapped, "Hurry up, I ain't got all day!"

Claudette began shaking her head. "No, absolutely not. I am not undressing in front of you."

He shrugged his shoulders. "Suit yourself, I don't care if you stay in those dirty rags, but the boss says I got to watch you, so I got to watch you."

"Can we come to some kind of compromise?"

"Such as?"

She racked her brain trying to think of something she thought he would agree to. "How about I sing while I'm bathing, then you can hear me and know I'm not wandering off."

He considered for a moment and then nodded. "All right, but you so much as change pitch or volume and I'm looking."

She nodded. "Deal." He moved a few paces away and turned slightly so that she was just a little behind his shoulder. She hesitated a moment trying to think of a song. Her mind was completely blank. She began muttering to herself as she tried to think of a song. While she undressed, she kept saying, "I'm thinking, I'm thinking."

After about the fifteenth time she had said 'I'm thinking', Jake replied with irritation, "This was your idea."

"Well, excuse me, my mind is completely blank or I can only think of one verse. And I don't think you want to hear the same verse five hundred times … oh, wait, I thought of something." She finished undressing, took a deep breath then started singing. "I've been the wild rover for many a year. And I've spent all me money on whiskey and beer. But now I'm returning with gold in great store. And I never will play the wild rover no more. And it's no, nay, never; no, nay, never no more. Will I play the wild rover, no, never, no more." While she had been singing, she slipped into the pond and began washing.

Jake could not help himself. When she started singing, he looked over his shoulder to stare at her. That was not what he had expected a proper young lady to sing. She had her back turned to him and she was standing a little deeper than her waist, splashing water on herself. As she began lathering her body with soap, he momentarily forgot that he was supposed to be a gentleman and should not be staring at her, nevertheless, he continued to stare at her naked back a moment longer as he listened to her sing. She had a lovely singing voice. He thought he could listen to her all day.

Claudette interrupted her singing momentarily to say, "I'm getting my hair wet so you won't be hearing me singing, but you'll definitely be hearing me splash."

Jake quickly looked away. Despite his best efforts to behave like a gentleman, he snuck several peeks. He had done this five times without getting caught, but when he glanced back this time, she was just turning and saw him. She quickly covered her breasts and dropped down into the water. She said angrily, "You pervert!" She cupped her hand and propelled it quickly forward, sending a spray of water across him.

When they entered the shack a few minutes later, Frank demanded, "How did you get wet?"

Jake opened his mouth to reply, but Claudette got there first. "He forgot to be a gentleman and looked, so I splashed him."

All of the men erupted into laughter. Frank walked over and patted him on the back. "Well, I have to admit, I didn't think you had it in you."

Jake said with irritation, "Shut up, Frank." Then he moved towards his bunk, lay down, and laid his arm over his eyes.

Claudette looked around. "Let me guess, the prisoner is supposed to prepare dinner?"

Sam replied, "That depends if you wanted edible or not."

She quickly held up both hands. "No, no, I'll cook, that's okay, thank you." As she went about cooking, she took this opportunity to study Sam and Walt. Walt seemed to be the oldest of the bunch, close to forty, but he gave her the impression of the meek, whiny follower type. He was of average height, a little heavyset with mouse brown hair and brown eyes, not particularly good looking. Sam was a rather tall, good looking black man in his early twenties, broadly built with a shaved head. He seemed to have a watchful, wary nature. Any time anybody moved, he twitched and he immediately looked to see what was going on. He was going to be the one to make it especially hard for her to escape. She would have to find a way around him.

    Jake lay on his bunk pretending to sleep, but he shifted his arm so he could discreetly watch the girl. He did not think for a minute Claudette was really her name. She just did not look like a Claudette. She was tall, five foot seven or so, eighteen or nineteen, very slender with dark brown hair that hung to her waist and very green eyes, and she was far too pretty for her own good, or his for that matter. This was definitely going to complicate matters.

V

Claudette considered her escape while she was preparing dinner. She would not be able to make her escape on foot, but there was a stable with horses just next door; and they were not exactly quiet horses, which was to her advantage. She also had on good walking shoes, not ideal for horseback riding, but better than dress shoes and her skirt would easily allow her to ride astride. These were all good things. She also had her derringer. Food was not an issue, as she was no more than a few hours ride from help. This was in her part of Texas. She had grown up out here and felt comfortable riding off into the dark by herself. She considered for a moment. To find all of the accouterments and saddle the horse should not take her any longer than ten minutes, it was a small stable. And twenty minutes head start should make it impossible for them to find her. Half an hour, she needed to find a way to carve out a half an hour in the middle of the night. That was going to be difficult, but as of yet, she had given them no trouble. She did not think they were going to tie her up. She would just have to watch and see. She should not attempt anything tonight, they would expect it. She would have to wait and see how tomorrow played out. She finished preparing dinner, then they all ate, and she cleaned up. To her relief, they did not tie her up, though Frank did establish watches.

In the morning, she checked on her patient, who seemed to be doing well. He was sitting up with help and was in good spirits. That was another relief, at least Frank was not going to kill her for failing to save his brother. Sadly, no one strayed far from the shack, making it impossible for her to try anything during the day. She was careful to do nothing to cause them any alarm. She was also careful to never stray near the stables and give them any ideas. After dinner, everyone went to bed. She had listened carefully, but tonight Frank did not establish watches. She lay on the floor wrapped up in a blanket pretending to sleep. She was sure it was now near midnight. She got up very quietly and picked up her shoes and tiptoed out of the shack. Once outside she slipped her shoes on, then moved carefully to the stables. She was only a few feet away when a figure loomed out of the darkness. He grabbed her and pressed her into the side of the stables, his forearms pressed against the wall of the stables, pinning her arms to her side. As he pressed his body tightly against hers, she opened her mouth to protest. He kissed her. She was so startled, it took a moment before she realized who it was, but the mustache told her it could only be Frank. She squirmed for a moment, then was able to pull her mouth free. She said with irritation, "Get your hands off me!"

Frank chuckled softly. "My hands aren't on you, they could be if you would like them, but where exactly did you think you were going?"

She squirmed against him, but he pressed her tighter into the side of the stables. "I was going to the privy. Now let me go."

He kissed her again and rubbed his body into hers, then he pulled his mouth free. "Don't leave the shack again without permission or we might just get the idea you're trying to run away." He stepped back and allowed her to head in the direction of the privy. He struck a match on the side of the stables, then lit a cigarette as he watched her go. He chuckled to himself. He did not believe her for a minute.

Claudette walked towards the privy, feeling Frank's eyes on her every step of the way. She must have rushed things. Maybe she should have waited longer. She sighed. Now he was going to watch her even more intently. She had blown her one chance. What an idiot she had been. She would ask in the morning how much longer they were going to hold her. She was terrified of the answer, but not knowing was worse.

After breakfast the following morning, Claudette looked at Frank and asked a little nervously, "How much longer are you going to hold me? What are you going to do with me?"

All eyes turned to stare at Frank. He cleared his throat and replied, "As of right now, my plan is to hold onto you until we change hideouts. At that time, we'll put you on one of the spare horses and point you in the direction of the nearest town and we can part company. After all, I do owe you one for savin' my little brother's life, but if you give us any trouble, I might have to re-evaluate that decision."

Claudette considered that for a long moment. "I guess under the circumstances, that is more than fair. When do you anticipate changing hideouts?"

"Couple weeks."

Her jaw dropped and she stared and stammered out, "A coup ... couple ... of we ... eks?"

"That's what I said, but if you like our company, we can always keep you with us."

She started sniffing and put her hand to her mouth. She was quite certain she was going to burst into tears any minute. She did not think she could endure this for a couple of weeks. She wanted to go home. She wanted to see her mother and father. She wanted to sit in her own parlor with her friends and family around her. She decided she would not allow Frank to see her cry. She turned and stormed out of the shack, heading for the well. When she arrived, she gripped the side of it and started sobbing. After a couple of minutes, she felt a hand on the small of her back. She jumped and pulled away as she looked to see who was standing there. Jake offered her a handkerchief. She took it and said grudgingly, "Thank you."

"I know this ain't easy, but a couple weeks ain't the end of the world. It will fly by."

She wiped her eyes and sniffed. "Oh yes, I'm sure the time is going to go so quickly, cooking and cleaning up after you lot." She sniffed several more times.

Jake tried to conceal a smile as he said gently, "Go ahead and blow your nose."

She hesitated only a moment before she carefully blew her nose. After a moment she said, "I'll wash it for you."

"That's very kind of you, but I can do my own laundry, thank you." Seeing that she looked calmer, he reached over and took his handkerchief back and stuck it in his pocket. "It'll be all right. I know Frank's a bit rough around the edges, but he ain't the worst person in the world."

She momentarily contemplated replying that yes, he definitely was not a bad guy. He just pinned innocent girls to the wall and kissed them against their will in the dark of night, but she decided Jake probably would not give her any sympathy. It also probably would not do her reputation any good if it got around that an outlaw had kissed her, so she decided it was best if she forgot such a thing had happened. "Yes, I'm sure he's one of the most charming outlaws in Texas."

Jake chuckled. "I guarantee you he ain't even close to the worst."

Frank interrupted them. "Jake, bring her back inside and tie her to one of the bunks."

Claudette's eyes widened and she gave a little screech. "What? No!"

She turned and tried to flee, but Jake grabbed her around the waist, picked her up, and carried her inside. He sat her on one of the bottom bunks and demanded, "Why are we tying her up?"

"Because we have a noon appointment in Lefors. Now tie her up so we can get out of here. Tie her hands to the top bunk, it will make it more difficult for her to try anything." Frank turned to Sam and gestured. "You're staying behind. You look after her and my brother, and remember, if she gets away, we all swing."

Sam grumbled but nodded. "As long as I don't gotta like it. Ain't right kidnapping a young girl, holding her prisoner. Her family must be scared to death."

Frank snorted. "Quit your complaining. We ain't hurting her and we'll send her on her way soon enough, none the worse for wear."

Claudette struggled while Jake tried to tie her hands to the side railing of the upper bunk. Finally he snapped, "Dammit, woman, stop it! You're making this worse on yourself. The more you struggle, the more it's gonna hurt. Just let me tie your hands and be done with it. We'll be back in a couple hours and we'll untie you."

She stopped struggling and let him tie her hands, then they all left except Sam and José. After a few minutes, José said apologetically, "I'm very sorry. My brother can be difficult sometimes, but he will not hurt you."

She snorted and replied with irritation, "Really, right now I feel very hurt. This isn't very comfortable. And after sitting here for several hours with my arms over my head, tied to a board, I know I'm going to be hurting."

"I know. I'm sorry, but Frank would be very cross if we untied you. He thinks you will give him trouble."

She rolled her eyes and refrained from commenting that these men did not know what trouble was. They had now gone against her parents, and her parents were not going to like that, and if they kept true to form, either her father and his men would come after her, or they would hire someone to get her back – and her parents only hired the best.

VI

Lefors, Texas
Monday, July 2, 1906

Frank casually surveyed the area as he and Walt rode into town. Jake and Kenny were going to arrive a few minutes later from the other side of town. Everything looked nice and quiet. Nobody seemed on the alert. He came to a stop outside the Gunderson Bank, dismounted, and threw his reins over the hitching post. Walt did the same, then Frank bent down and gripped the rear leg of his horse and lifted it up. He examined it for a moment, then pulled out his knife and pretended as though he was prying a stone loose. Walt said softly, "Kenny and Jake are headed this way. Ain't fifty feet behind us."

Frank nodded, released the leg of his horse, stood up and patted him on the rump, murmuring softly, "There now buddy, I bet that feels a whole lot better." He patted his horse gently several more times, then turned and headed for the bank. As they entered, they pulled their bandannas up to cover their faces.

As the teller looked up from behind the counter, his smile died on his lips. "Good afternoon, gentlemen. I hope there's not going to be any trouble. We'll cooperate fully, there's no need for violence."

Walt paused by the door and flicked the open sign to closed, just as Kenny entered, closing the door behind him. Frank said deliberately, a little breathless and with a very bad Spanish accent, "I am quite glad to hear it, Señor. We no want any bloodshed, so just hand over all the money in the drawer. Manuel, go into the safe. Fernando, make sure the manager does cause no trouble."

Kenny decided for the day he was apparently Manuel and went to empty the safe, leaving Walt to be Fernando. He did not know why, but occasionally Frank got these fanciful ideas and liked to use accents during a robbery and give false names. He apparently found it amusing. Most of the time it did not bother anyone, but occasionally he would give ridiculous names that would irritate one of the gang, like the time he decided they were all going to have girls names. He was sure the only thing that had stopped Sam from killing him was the fact that he had given himself a girl's name too. He had been Francesca. Kenny snickered as he remembered. Frank moved forward and began grabbing the money off the counter while watching the teller. Walt returned from tying up and disarming the manager. He proceeded to tie up the teller, who was not carrying a gun. However, he did notice a gun next to the teller's drawer. He picked it up and dumped the bullets out, then proceeded to disassemble the gun, leaving it in three pieces. Kenny was just coming out of the safe when there was a knock on the door. Clearly something had caused Jake to become nervous.

They all turned and headed quickly for the door. As they exited the bank, bags in hand, a few people were staring. It was not until they mounted up and turned their horses that someone screamed, "They just robbed the bank!"

Frank nudged his horse and headed down the alley. "This way, boys!" They followed him and though they heard a few shots, none of them hit home and a few minutes later they were well away. Frank laughed and pulled his bandanna down. "Well, boys, a few more hauls like that and I think we can settle down and buy a little piece of land, maybe in Colorado."

Kenny laughed. "Farming is for the old. I intend to spend my money and start all over." He hooted with laughter.

Walt shook his head. "I'm with Frank. A nice, quiet little place, find me a wife and have some kids. I'm getting too old for this. What about you, Jake?"

"I think the life I've chosen doesn't exactly leave room for a wife and kids, and it sure as hell ain't ever going to be quiet. Somebody's always gonna be shootin' at me and they say old sins cast long shadows. Which I guess that means things always come back around and you can never get away from them."

Frank snorted and shook his head. "You are so melancholy for one so young and since you're not exactly the wife for a night kind like Kenny, we all know you'll find yourself a little Missus, settle down, and raise fat babies."

Jake decided there was no arguing with them. He would just keep his peace.

*****

Claudette's arms were sore, but not nearly as sore as her temper. She must have been sitting like this for three or four hours and she was becoming increasingly alarmed by the way Sam kept looking at her. He got to his feet and poured a glass of water and brought it over. "Thirsty?"

"That would require you untying my hands." He moved to press the glass to her lips. She pulled her head away. "No, thank you. I'll wait."

"What? You won't take it from me because I'm a colored man?"

She sighed and looked annoyed. "One has nothing to do with the other. I don't like anyone feeding me. Even when I was a child and sick, I didn't like for my mother to feed me, or even to give me my medicine. I always preferred to do it myself. And anyways, since you won't untie me, I don't think drinking anything right now is a very good idea."

He shrugged his shoulders. "Probably true." He sat on the edge of the bunk and continued to stare at her. After a moment, he reached out and rubbed his knuckle across her cheek.

She pulled her head away and said, "Don't touch me."

"You know, you're an awfully pretty thing and you're real kind and you're a good cook. You'll make some man a fine wife one day."

She said coldly, "Well that man won't be you." He opened his mouth, but she cut him off. "Don't you dare say it's because you're a colored man. One has nothing to do with the other."

"So you say you'd marry a colored man?"

She considered that for a moment, and then shook her head. "No, I don't believe I would. To begin with, it is illegal, and I'm a law-abiding citizen. If I were to meet a colored man and fall in love with him, I would probably insist that we move to France where it is not illegal, but that would involve alienating myself from my family permanently, and I don't think I'm willing to do that."

"Yeah, your Pa wouldn't like you marrying a black man."

"My father is a very open and loving man, but no, I don't think he would. Nor would my Uncle

Leopold or my Uncle Carlos. The world we live in just isn't ready for that. Maybe one day, but this is not that day."

"Carlos? You got a Mexican uncle? You don't look like you got Mexican blood."

She sighed. "All of the ranchers grew up together. My father and Uncle Carlos and some of the other boys were always thick as thieves ..." She grimaced over her choice of wording, shrugged her shoulders, and went on. "... growing up. Uncle Leopold started working with them before I was born. He's a black man. I've known him all my life and I've called him Uncle Leopold all my life. There are quite a few of the hands who've known my Mama and Daddy since before I was born. I remember many a time getting in trouble with Uncle Leopold and him putting me over his knee and paddling my backside, and then taking me home where my Daddy did it again."

Sam stared at her in amazement. "Your Daddy let a colored man spank his daughter?"

She sighed again. "I don't think it ever entered my parents' heads to protest. They were more irritated with whatever I had done wrong. Now don't get me wrong, there were some around the ranch my father would not have been so accepting of them punishing me. But that had to do with how much he did not trust them." She hesitated a moment and then shook her head. "Why is this even a subject of discussion? You are a criminal."

"I won't always be a criminal."

She shook her head firmly. "That is where we disagree most strongly. You clearly have the attitude of a criminal, and will always be a criminal unless you choose to change your behavior; which at this time I don't see that happening, because you prefer to make easy money rather than work hard."

Sam growled and got to his feet. José realized too late that he was going to strike her. He winced as her head snapped back, but only as far as her bonds would let her. Sam brought his hand back to strike her again. José struggled to get to his feet but was unable to. He said weakly, "Touch her again and Frank will shoot you."

Sam turned and glared at him. "You stay out of this." He grabbed her around the waist and jerked her towards him. "You think you're better than me. You're not. You're just some prissy, whiny little brat, who doesn't know anything. Someday somebody's gonna teach you a lesson, and if I'm lucky, it'll be me." He kissed her roughly. She bit his lip. "Ow! Dammit, that hurt, you little brat!" Then he let her go and backhanded her several times, turned, and stormed out.

When Frank returned an hour later, he saw immediately that Sam's horse was missing from the stables. He frowned and headed for the shack. When he entered, he could see that Claudette had been crying and looked a little banged up. José was lying on the floor. He demanded, "What in God's name happened here?" He moved towards his brother, picked him up, and put him back on his bunk.

Jake had entered behind Frank and moved to Claudette. He could see a good size bruise forming on her right cheek, and she had clearly been fighting against her bonds. He realized immediately she had made the knot too tight. He pulled his knife and went to cut her bonds. She screeched and tried to pull her hands away. He said angrily, "Stop struggling." He cut her free.

José said weakly, "Sam took her some water. She wouldn't drink it. They disagreed, not argued, just disagreed. He showed his interest. She told him exactly what she thought of all of us. It wasn't very favorable. He became angry and struck her. I told him you would kill him if he didn't stop. They argued a little and he struck her several more times, then he left. He has been gone more than an hour."

Jake growled and retrieved a bucket of cold water and a cloth, saying with irritation, "Walt, get her some coffee and put a little whiskey in it."

"I'm fine, and why are you always trying to put whiskey in me? It's a vile drink."

"Because it's good for shock and it's good for calming nerves and yours look about shattered." He began gently applying the cool, damp cloth to the side of her face. There was a little blood, but he could not see where it had come from, probably the inside of her mouth. When he was finished with her face, Walt handed him a coffee cup. He took it and took a big swig. "Put some more whiskey in it." Walt grabbed the bottle and poured. "That's enough." He pressed it into her hands, pointed and ordered, "Drink it all."

"No."

He glowered at her. "Drink the coffee of your own will or I'll make you drink straight from the bottle again. The choice is yours. One way or another, it's going down."

She glared at him but drank it down in one pull. She immediately felt a little dizzy. She demanded, "Are you sure there was any coffee in there?"

He took the empty cup from her hands and murmured, "Not much." Then he retrieved the cloth and began cleaning up her wrists. He growled again. Her wrists looked pretty bad. "Dammit, woman, I tied you up carefully. Why did you have to fight your bonds so hard for?"

"I'm sorry, but José tried to get up out of bed and fell. I was trying to get over to help him. He could not get back up. I was afraid he might pop the stitches and bleed to death and there would be nothing I could do to help him." She turned to Frank and demanded, "What do his bandages look like? Is he bleeding?" Her words seemed to be slurring just a little.

Frank carefully examined his brother's front and back. There were only a couple of little spots of dried blood. "Nope, they seem to have held."

Claudette sighed with relief. She leaned back against the pillow and murmured, "Thank God for that."

Jake snorted and said with irritation, "Kenny, bring me my saddlebags." Kenny did as he was told and Jake began rooting around. He pulled out a tin of utter butter.

"You know, this is not necessary. I can look after myself."

He ignored her and began applying it liberally to her wrists, then carefully bandaged them. When he was finished, he wrung out the cloth and gently applied it to her cheek. "Ruddy bastard better hope I don't lay eyes on him again."

She took the cloth from him and held it to her cheek. "Thank you, I can do that." She did not know what was wrong with her. Her body felt very weird and she could barely keep her eyes open. She demanded, "What did you put in the whiskey?"

Jake wanted to argue, but it was probably best if he worked on keeping his distance. He got to his feet and murmured, "Just whiskey, go to sleep, lightweight." Her body went completely limp a moment later. He wandered over to the other side of the room.

"Psst, psst." went José.

Jake turned to stare at the kid. He demanded softly, "What?"

José whispered softly, "Don't look at me. I don't want Frank to notice."

Jake demanded under his breath, "Then why are you talking to me?"

"We have to keep an eye on the señorita. She is too pretty. Sam tried to kiss her and she bit him. I think Frank has eyes for her too. He's always watching her."

Jake growled and murmured, "Not my problem."

VII

Claudette was not sure how long she had been asleep, but she had now been awake, sitting in moody silence for nearly an hour, contemplating if she was ever going to see home again, when her brain slowly became aware of something her ears had heard a minute or two earlier; horses, and lots of them. It only took her mind a moment to form the thought, *A posse.* She closed her eyes and began praying that the men would have the good sense to surrender without a fight.

Frank said quickly, "Shut up everyone. Do you hear that?"

Jake groaned. "Posse. I told you we came back here too directly."

Walt got up and glanced out the window. "Shit! It ain't Frank's fault. Fucking Sam sold us out! I can see his stupid ass from here."

"How close are they?" demanded Frank.

"Close enough you can spit on him if you wanna. They got us blocked off from that direction, but from how many there are out there, something tells me they ain't got us surrounded."

Frank growled, opened his mouth to speak, but a voice from outside hollered, "This is the Lefors Sheriff. You have to the count of twenty to throw out your guns and come out with your hands up, or we open fire! 1 … 2 …"

Frank turned and hissed at Jake. "Take José and the girl and get out of here. We'll cover you."

Jake nodded and kicked over the table, then threw back the rug to reveal a trap door. Walt hopped down and Jake grabbed José and lowered him down to Walt. Claudette said with irritation, "No, I'm not going with you! I'm going home with the posse."

Jake sighed with irritation, grabbed her arm, and yanked her towards the trap door. She opened her mouth to scream and he put his hand over her mouth as he struggled to get ahold of her. Once he had one arm around her waist and the other clamped tightly over her mouth, he said angrily in her ear, "And exactly how are you going to get out of this shack alive after they pump hundreds of rounds of lead into it?"

To prove his point, the Sheriff said, "… 19 … 20. Open fire, boys!" Jake took her to the floor and covered her with his body. She did not argue as they scrambled behind the table, then dropped into the cellar.

Jake demanded, "José, Walt, where are you?"

Walt shouted to be heard over the gunfire, "Probably about halfway down the passage. Hurry."

Claudette felt like screaming as she heard dozens, if not hundreds of gunshots above her. She and Jake headed into a narrow passage that she could not see but could feel. She bumped into Walt with his arm around José. The four of them hurried ahead. She ran into a wall and began feeling around. Finding a ladder, she started up. It was much quieter over here. She could hear someone just entering the other side of the tunnel. Kenny said, "I closed and barred the trap door. That should slow them down for a few minutes." She finished scrambling up the ladder and pushed open a trap door. As soon as she was off the ladder, she turned back to help pull José up, as the others pushed him.

Jake replied with irritation as he shoved José up, "Let's just hope they're not big enough bastards to have fired into the stables." When José was off the ladder, the others scrambled up behind him.

Frank, Jake, and Kenny quickly began saddling the horses. Walt cautiously peeped out of a knothole, then he whispered as he moved towards his own horse. "We better hurry. Some of them are heading into the shack. The others seem to be reloading.

Claudette, seriously wondering what she was about, saddled a horse for José. She glanced at Frank. He was mumbling to himself as he was saddling his horse. It took her a moment to process what he was saying. He was counting in Spanish, "75 ... 76 ... 77 ... 78 ..."

Jake quickly checked the horse she was saddling, then grabbed her, picked her up in his arms and threw her on his horse and mounted up behind her, while Frank helped José into the saddle, then mounted up himself. The others were already mounted. She started to scream and struggle, but Jake clamped his hand firmly over her mouth and said in her ear, "If you don't want to end up dead, shut yer damn mouth."

Then they all burst out of the rear door of the stables. A few stray bullets were fired at them and someone from the posse yelled, "They're getting away!"

Frank shouted, "... 85 ... 86 ..." Then there was a large explosion. Claudette screamed.

Walt demanded, "Sounds like you lost count. Do you think you got any of the posse in the explosion?"

Frank shrugged his shoulders and replied, "If we are lucky, no. And no, I think in my excitement I counted irregularly, though it is possible the fuse did not burn quite right. They can be a little irregular sometimes. It happens."

Claudette struggled and said angrily, "Let me go! This is a wonderful opportunity for you to be rid of me and me to be free of you."

Jake said with irritation, "Shut up and quit your bitching or I'll gag you."

She clapped her mouth shut but looked over her shoulder and glared at him. They spent what she guessed was about the next three hours riding, cutting trails, backtracking, heading down streams, then backtracking. She felt dizzy. She just was not sure whether it was from the whiskey, fear, or all the backtracking. They had all been making various threats on Sam's life. He better hope he never ran across one of them again. It sounded as though none of them would kill him quickly. When Frank finally decided they were safe and could camp for the night, Jake lowered her off the horse. She rubbed her back and glared at him. "I hate you. Why couldn't you let me go?"

Jake growled, grabbed her by the arm and dragged her little way from the others, then slammed her back into a tree and glared down at her. "Ain't you never heard of a lynch mob? Most posses are little better than that. They're angry men drunk on power and they don't care who they hurt. There are more than a few posses and sheriffs who've killed dozens of innocent people to catch one guilty man, and if you were lucky, that's what they would've done to you, pump you full of lead and left you there, but posses often have a lot worse in mind for pretty young ladies. And there is a very good chance that they wouldn't believe that we kidnapped you and after they were done doing whatever they were gonna do, they'd either throw you in jail till your parents convinced them otherwise, or just shoot you and bury you in a shallow grave. A posse is never a good thing."

She stared up at him, opening and closing her mouth several times, trying to find something to say. Finally she faltered and looked down and murmured, "I'm sure all criminals think that everyone is as bad as they are, but I'm sure the Sheriff would not have allowed such a thing to happen."

He gripped her chin and forced her to look at him. "Lefors doesn't have a Sheriff right now. They rely on the Texas Rangers. So any man who begins with a lie is not a man to be trusted. Those men were definitely acting outside the law, and a group like that is more likely to kill any and all witnesses, then divide up the haul and claim they never found anything. You are far too trusting."

She replied with a shaky voice, "Well, perhaps the man who was speaking was a Texas Ranger …"

Jake cut her off. "No Texas Ranger would claim to be a mere Sheriff." He grabbed her by the arm and dragged her back to the encampment.

Frank demanded as they approached, "Jake, you know this area better than anyone else, are there any farms or ranches nearby where we can steal some horses?"

"We may be able to steal some horses from the Lazy Leaf Ranch, but we'll have to be really careful. They're a large outfit."

"How close is the ranch house?" asked Frank.

"Not real sure. Ain't never been there. Ain't never even met them. They use Donegal for all their needs. My daddy went to Pampa for whatever we needed, but you don't live up here and not know about the McLoughlins. Like I said, they're a huge outfit, employ something like thirty men."

"Yes, yes, I've heard of them. We will definitely want to stay clear of them. We don't want to cause them any trouble."

"You don't want to cause people trouble, but you'll steal their horses?" snapped Claudette.

"I don't steal from those who can't afford it, and if they're as big an outfit as he says they are, they won't miss a few horses."

Claudette refrained from comment. She knew her daddy would. So would Uncle Leopold, Uncle Lonnie, Uncle Carlos, and Joey. They noticed when a calf went missing out of thousands of head of cattle. They would notice a few horses. Deciding he was not worth arguing with, she went to check on José.

"I think it's best if we borrow our horses from someone other than the McLoughlins. We'll find somewhere else, someone who won't notice a few horses missing for a few days. But all that can wait until morning and then it'll be safe to put her on a horse and send her to Pampa. Then she's out of our hair and we can get back to business."

Jake and Walt nodded in agreement.

Frank waited until Walt wandered off, then he moved over to Jake and gently elbowed him in the side. "So is that what it takes to rouse your desire, a few gunshots? She's quite a good little kisser an' she and that body of hers is nice and soft, nice to rub up against isn't it?"

Jake turned quickly and grabbed Frank's shirt with both hands, moved in close, and growled in his face, "You keep your damn hands off of her, or I'll have to teach you a lesson."

Frank shoved against him saying as he did so, "Who the hell do you think you are? Get your hands off me."

"You told me to make sure no one messed with her. Touch her again and I'll wipe the floor with you. Is that clear?"

Frank started laughing, then asked, "Guess that means you didn't get kissy kissy with her in the woods."

Jake growled and slugged him, then turned and stormed off. Frank staggered back, hooted with laughter, and rubbed his face. Jake was awful fun to get under his skin. It was such an easy thing to do. He wiggled his jaw back and forth, then grumbled, "Awww." Okay, maybe this time had not been quite as much fun, at least the getting hit part was not. The man had a right like a sledgehammer. Fortunately, he had pulled his punch at the last minute, otherwise Frank would have been eating dirt. He wandered over to the girl. He did not know why, but he refused to think of her as Claudette. It just did not suit her. Though she was exquisitely beautiful with a lovely body, there just seemed to be something so down-to-earth and practical about her. It almost ruined the whole effect. It was almost like she should have been named Beth. She was examining his brother's wound. He demanded, "How's he doing?"

She did not bother to look up as she replied, "Surprisingly enough, healing rather nicely. I think he will be able to ride in a couple of days if you don't get him shot again or hung in the meantime."

Frank shook his head. "You know, Missy, with that smart mouth of yours, you'll have a hard time finding a husband despite all your good looks. You might work on a vacant smile. Men find that more appealing."

She snorted and shook her head. "If a man wants a halfwit for a wife, I'm not the right woman for him. I don't back down and I stand up for what I believe." She got to her feet and shook out her skirts, then said coldly, "Good night, Mr. Ramirez."

VIII

Claudette shifted and stirred, then sat up in bed and looked around. It took her a full minute to realize where she was, she was home. She smiled and lay back down and snuggled into the covers. It was so good to be home. She lay there for a few more minutes, then she got up, got dressed, and headed downstairs. She peeked into her father's office, it was empty. She frowned, then she headed into the kitchen. She sighed with exasperation. Her mother must be out somewhere. She murmured to herself with some disappointment, "That's the problem with ranch life, life continues to go on. I haven't even been home one day and they're all out. Oh well, I guess I can go for a ride. I didn't need to have breakfast anyway."

She was glad she had decided to put on her riding skirt. She crossed to the rifle stand and pulled her rifle down, then checked to see if it was loaded. She frowned. That was odd. She could have sworn that before she had gone away to school she had unloaded her rifle, cleaned it, and put it away. She murmured to herself, "Maybe Daddy had loaded it in anticipation of my coming home." She shrugged her shoulders dismissively, grabbed a box of ammunition, and headed to the stables and in no time at all, she was riding across the open fields, heading for the small rifle range her father had built some years back. She was really looking forward to practicing her shooting. She had not fired a gun in years. Arriving at the little makeshift range, she dismounted and threw the reins over the little hitching post. She pulled the box of ammunition out of her saddle bag and moved to the little table. She stared at it in amazement. It looked exactly as it had four years ago, nothing had changed. She ran a finger along the table. It appeared to have been freshly painted. She opened the box of ammo and took a few practice shots. She was pleased to see her aim was as good as ever. A quarter of an hour later, she was just finishing loading her rifle for the third and final time, deciding that a half a box of ammunition was more than sufficient practice for this morning. She was startled by a voice from behind her.

A man said, "You shouldn't be out here all by yourself."

She turned quickly, then jumped back, tightening her grip on her rifle. A scuzzy looking saddle tramp was standing there. "Is there something I can help you with, sir?"

"I was looking for the ranch house. I heard they might be hiring for the round up. You know, little girls shouldn't be playing with rifles." He took two steps closer to her.

She stepped back and bumped into the table. It fell over. Hearing the ammunition spill, she looked over her shoulder. He stepped forward quickly and grabbed her rifle, trying to wrench it from her hands. As she struggled to hold onto the rifle, she started screaming.

"Claudette." A voice from faraway called.

She screamed and struggled to hold onto the rifle, then it felt like her whole body was shaking. She screamed and screamed as everything around her started running like wet paint, the images blurring together.

Jake gently placed his hand over her mouth as he shook her again, saying gently, "It's just a bad dream. Wake up." Her eyes opened and she came back to reality with a crash. She pulled away, tried to get to her feet, then got tangled up in the blankets and flailed against him. Jake grabbed both of her forearms and said calmly, "Calm down, it's me, Jake. The others will hear you. You're safe. Please stop struggling."

She started murmuring and blubbering and then yanked her arms free and threw them around his neck, hugging him tightly. He hesitated a moment before gently wrapping his arms around her. With one hand, he rubbed up and down her back. She sobbed out, "Don't leave me alone."

Jake continued to gently rub his hand up and down her back and said softly, "It's all right. It was just a dream. You're safe now. It was just a bad dream." She shook her head fiercely against his chest. He tried to push her to arms reach, but she would not loosen her grip. After a minute he asked, "What happened?"

Claudette was still shaking like a leaf and sobbing. She could not get his face out of her mind. A part of her wanted to tell Jake, but the other part of her knew telling him was a really bad idea, so she clung to him tighter and shook her head again. "None of your business."

He tried again to push her to arms reach, but she tightened her grip around his neck and buried her face in his neck. She was now practically sitting on his lap. The harder he tried to push her away, the tighter she pressed against him. "Claudette, it was just a dream. Maybe if you talk about it, you'll feel better."

She sniffed several times and then said through her tears, "I'm not telling you anything."

He growled, gripped her arms, and tried to pull them from around his neck. "Well, if you don't want to talk to me, then I want to go back to sleep."

She screeched and clung tighter saying, "Please, no, don't leave me alone!"

He sighed and shifted from the awkward position he was in on one knee with her somehow tucked inside his arms, onto his backside with her curled up on his lap. She clung to him tightly crying, then her sobbing started to cease, and her grip loosened. He waited another couple of minutes. When he decided she had cried herself to sleep, he tried to pull her arms from around his neck, but she immediately tightened her grip and started crying again. He tried twice more to disentangle himself from her, but every time she woke up and started crying again. Finally he gave up, shifted a little more, and then pulled the blanket around them both. He murmured in her ear, "You know, if that posse was to find us now, this wouldn't do your reputation any good." Then he fell asleep holding her.

Claudette shifted and stirred. Every bone in her body ached and her head was throbbing and she felt like she was twisted into the most peculiar position imaginable. She shifted again and tried to figure out how she had ended up so twisted. Her eyes felt so heavy she could not seem to open them. Then she realized she was half laying on top of something soft and warm. Her eyes flew open as she struggled to push herself to her knees. Jake groaned and grunted several times as she kneed him and elbowed him repeatedly. Frank and Kenny roared with laughter. Claudette, now on her knees, looked around and realized that she had practically slept on top of Jake and under the same blanket. She felt her face become as hot as fire. She looked down. Her clothes were a wrinkled mess and nearly as twisted as her body had felt. She tried to turn her back, but found that that was impossible, it was so stiff. She had to quickly adjust her blouse because part of her corset and camisole were showing. While she tried to straighten herself, Jake got to his feet and said angrily to Frank, "Don't you and Kenny have somewhere else to be?"

"We were just wondering how long you two were going to be so cozy," replied Kenny with a grin.

"Shut your mouth, Kenny, or I'm gonna have to flatten you."

Kenny took a drink from his coffee and said with amusement, "I just find it interesting that Frank was worried about me, and yet here you are sleeping with her."

Jake shoved Kenny. "Shut up. Nothing happened."

Frank took a drink from his coffee and nodded his head. "Yes, I'm quite sure you're right. Absolutely right, nothing happened."

Jake turned and glared at Frank, his tone was dripping in sarcasm. "Don't we all have something we need to be doing?"

Frank took another drink from his coffee deliberately, looking amused over the rim of his cup. Jake was getting angrier. "Well, if you can separate yourself from that filly, we can put her on a horse and get her out of here ... unless, of course, you decided that you're gonna keep her?"

Claudette finally felt that she was as decent looking as she was going to be and pushed herself to her feet and said with irritation, "No one's keeping me, and yes, I'd like a horse so I can get away from all of you."

Jake snapped with irritation, "I'll saddle her a horse, because the sooner she's gone the better for everybody." He stormed off and saddled his horse. When he brought his horse back, he said with irritation, "She can use my saddle, I can get another one."

She opened her mouth to speak, but before she had a chance, he grabbed her around the waist, picked her up, and plopped her on the horse. She had barely struggled her other leg over the saddle before he said with irritation, "Pampa is a couple hours ride that direction and remember what I said about posses." Again she opened her mouth to speak, but did not have a chance. He slapped the horse's backside and sent it catapulting forward.

IX

Pampa, Texas
Tuesday, July 3, 1906

Joey paced up and down the front entry of the hotel, fidgeting with his wedding ring, every few minutes pulling out his watch to check the time. He glanced at JR and Jeffrey. JR was struggling to read the newspaper, but he was clearly as anxious as Joey for news. They had learned, too late last night to go investigate, that a posse had attacked a small shack. Matt had gone to investigate early this morning, insisting that the three of them needed to stay here in case more news came in. He paused in his pacing and considered young Jeffrey, who was clearly struggling with how he was supposed to feel. Joey could not blame him. He was not even sixteen years old and had only been eleven when Claudette had left, and she had been more like a bossy older sister than a friend, but for JR and himself, she had been like a baby sister. The door to the hotel opened and Matt entered looking annoyed, his saddlebags thrown over his shoulder. All four of them converged in the middle of the room. Joey demanded, "Was it them? Do you know anything?"

Matt took off his hat and said, "I have two of my men trying to catch up with the posse, but I don't expect this group to see any reason. They're nothing more than a bunch of angry townsmen. I don't think they're going to give a damn that these guys might be the same ones who robbed the train and might have a kidnapped girl with them. Fortunately, from what I saw when I went through what was left of the shack, which wasn't a lot since somebody blew it up, there was most definitely not any bodies, however." He lowered the saddlebags and pulled a dress out of one of them, "There was this." He shook it out. "The fabric looks expensive. I don't think it was bought out here, looks too fashionable. Looks like something you would've bought in New York City." He held it up by the shoulders. "And the woman who wore it was a shade on the tall side, but slightly built."

JR took it and turned it over in his hands. "Got a lot of blood on it, but I don't see any rips or tears or gunshot wounds. That stupid escort that the school sent said she was covered in blood by the time she was taken off the train, and he said she'd been wearing a green dress." Joey nodded in agreement.

The hotel manager approached. He cleared his throat. "I do understand the predicament you gentlemen are in, but that garment could upset my patrons. Do you mind putting it away?"

Matt took it and crammed it in the saddlebag, saying as he did so, "And one of my men learned that the same day as the train robbery, a Mexican man was in Lefors and bought a skirt and a blouse for woman. According to the shopkeeper, it was clearly something he'd never done before and he kept looking at them trying to decide if they were the right size."

Joey pursed his lips as he tried to think. "That makes sense. I mean, if you need her to keep your little brother alive, you'd want to be nice to her. I think you would buy her a new dress. You wouldn't want her to stay covered in blood. That might not make her very amiable and you need her on your side."

Matt nodded and said with irritation, "I just can't figure out what the girl was thinking getting herself involved. Why on earth would she try to help with his wounds anyways?"

Joey and JR both shook their heads, but it was JR who spoke. "I know. I agree with you, but it doesn't surprise me. That's exactly the kind of thing Claudette would do, ever since that damn incident on the ranch."

Matt cocked his head to the side and asked, "What incident? Is it pertinent to the case?"

Joey shrugged his shoulders. "Probably not. She was about thirteen or so, she'd gone out to practice with her rifle early one Sunday afternoon. Her folks had gone to have tea with Sean and Ana. She decided to stay home. Ain't much to the story. A drifter approached her. They talked for a minute. He tried to take her rifle. They struggled. She kicked him in the knee or some such thing. He staggered back, went for the rifle again and she put two bullets in his chest, dropped the rifle, and ran home. By the time she got back to the ranch house, Uncle Caleb and Aunt Dani were already home. Uncle Caleb left her there with her Mama. He, Leopold, and I went out, loaded the body up, retrieved the rifle, went back to the ranch house, and she and Uncle Caleb went into town and handed the body over to Sheriff. Near as I remember, with the exception of a very stern lecture about droppin' her rifle, it was an open and closed case."

Matt shook his head and pinched the bridge of his nose. "Out of curiosity, was Henry still Sheriff?"

Joey shook his head. "No, Henry retired a year or two earlier and moved to San Antonio."

Matt nodded. "Well, at least it is good to see that Miss Claudette is made of the same sturdy metal as her mother."

Joey laughed. "You got that right, they are two tough ladies." He sighed and went back to fidgeting with his wedding ring. "Those bastards hurt her, you won't be able to stop us from hunting them down."

Matt reached out and patted the younger man on the shoulder, opened his mouth, but they were interrupted by a slight commotion on the street. All four men turned and headed for the door. Just as Matt was reaching for it, it opened. He blinked and stepped back, allowing a woman, who he was quite certain was Claudette McLoughlin, to enter. She only gave him the briefest of glances, then her eyes alighted on the three men with him. She hugged Joey quickly, then reached out with one arm and grabbed JR around the neck and pulled him towards her and Joey.

As Claudette embraced her two older cousins, or at least as she had always thought of them, her eyes alighted on the young man behind them who now towered over her. She murmured, "Oh dear God, please tell me that's not Jeffrey." Even as she said it, she knew it was a ridiculous hope. He was clearly his father's son. The resemblance between him and Uncle Leopold was uncanny. He grinned back at her. She stared at him a moment longer. He was tall and broad and very good looking. He was wearing boots and jeans and a red button-down shirt. He had close cropped hair and a charming smile. She released Joey and JR and hugged Jeffrey, who hugged her back.

Joey laughed. "Sorry to say, little cousin, but that is most definitely Jeffrey. I know he's got four inches on me these days."

JR started laughing and shaking his head. "In your dreams, Joey. You're what, five ten? He's like six four. He's got at least six inches on you, not that being taller than you is anything impressive. I mean, I'm taller than you. I mean, let's be honest, Claudette is almost taller than you."

Claudette had to put her hand over her mouth to conceal a smile. Joey was very sensitive about the fact that almost all of his little cousins were taller than him. When she could speak without laughing, she said, "JR, stop picking on Joey, respect your elders."

JR rolled his eyes. "He's like, all of four years older than me, so he ain't that elder."

Claudette could not help it, she kept looking from one to the other again. It had been so long since she had seen either one of them. She was looking for differences. JR did not look any different than the last time she had seen him, his shaggy blond hair hanging down to his collar, with dark blue eyes, wearing boots, jeans, and a hat. The only thing that was different was the last time she had seen him he'd been wearing a blue shirt, today he was wearing a green one. She shifted her gaze to Joey who was now wearing his black curly hair short and neatly kept. He was clean shaven and very good looking. She smiled. He was also wearing boots, jeans, and a light blue shirt, that was a sharp contrast to his dark brown skin. He looked so respectable. She reached up and fiddled with the back of his hair. "Lupe has definitely made some positive changes in your appearance. I almost feel like I should call you Mr. Alvarez."

Matt cleared his throat. "You'll forgive the interruption, Miss McLoughlin. I'm Matt Crawford of the Pinkerton National Detective Agency. I was hired by your parents to retrieve you. Perhaps we could go into the lounge and you can have something to eat and we can ask you some questions?"

She sighed. "Yes, of course, I'm sure that is most necessary."

Joey offered her his arm and escorted her into the lounge, which was empty. A waitress approached. "Is there something I can get you all?"

Matt turned to Claudette and asked, "What would you like?"

She blushed slightly. "I'm sorry to say I'm positively starving. Would some sandwiches be possible?"

Matt turned back to the waitress. "A tray of sandwiches, perhaps some cake, tea for the young lady, and I think us gentlemen would prefer beer."

Joey took Claudette's hand and squeezed it warmly. With his free hand, he reached up and tentatively touched her right cheek. "Which one of the dirty rats did that? You look tired, you gonna be all right? Did they feed you well enough?"

She smiled at him and squeezed his hand. "You can stop worrying. They treated me very well, given the circumstances. I would say the cruelest thing I was forced to endure was sleeping on the hardwood floor, the woods last night was better than the floor." She reached up and tentatively touched her cheek. "And in regards to that, believe it or not, there are five of them. If they get their hands on him, they'll kill him for you. The one called Sam did that, though Kenny did hit me on the train."

Joey sighed with relief. "I'm so relieved to hear that. I will be right back. I need to go and telegraph your parents that you're safe." He started to pull free, but she gripped his hand tighter. He looked down at her with concern.

She blushed slightly. "I'm sure it's silly, but please don't go."

Joey suddenly felt very concerned, but he seated himself and held onto her hand. He looked at Matt. "Do you have some paper? I can write off a telegraph and have someone from the hotel send it."

"Of course," replied Matt, producing a notebook from his pocket and handing it over.

It only took Joey a moment to write it. When the waitress returned with four beers and a pot of tea, he tore off the note and handed it to her, along with two dollars. "Can you please have someone from the hotel take this down to the telegraph office and have it sent immediately. And then can you let the hotel manager know that we would like a hot bath taken to room five."

"Yes, sir, right away."

Claudette knew she was being silly, but she did not know Mr. Crawford and she just did not think she could handle being questioned by him alone. And as far as JR was concerned, she just had not ever been as close to him, and Jeffrey, well, she viewed him as a boy. She just preferred Joey not to leave her. She poured herself some tea, still refusing to let go of Joey's hand while she discreetly studied Mr. Crawford. He was about forty, with brown hair just starting to turn gray, brown eyes that seemed to notice everything, and was watching her intently. He was tall, slender, nice looking, but not handsome. He seemed friendly enough, but something told her he was not the kind of man to cross.

Joey found his concern was growing. This did not seem like Claudette at all. She seemed her happy normal self when she first entered the hotel, but now with every passing moment she seemed to be shrinking and her grip on his hand was getting tighter. He exchanged worried looks with Matt.

Matt decided to remain silent until the food had arrived and they could talk in relative privacy. Once everyone had a plate with sandwiches on it, he asked gently, "We have several accounts of the train robbery, but we would like to hear your version of events, please."

Claudette nodded and carefully went over everything up to the point where she exited the train. Her nervousness increased as Mr. Crawford made notes, occasionally making noises, or he would say things like, 'ah yes', 'I see', or 'interesting'.

Matt nodded. "Yes, that's all very clear now. Thank you. What happened after that?"

She hesitated a long moment, deciding what she was going to say about everything else. She decided that it was best if she stuck to the facts and left out any of her own thoughts or feelings. She also decided it was best to leave out any of the incidences where Jake forced liquor on her. Those might be misinterpreted, and it was also best to leave out bathing and Frank kissing her, and of course the fact that she apparently fell asleep in Jake's arms last night, or this morning, or whenever it was. She took another moment to gather her thoughts, then she said a little uncertainly, "There's really not a lot to tell. We arrived outside a shack. I finished attending to the boy José's wounds, then they took him inside. The one in charge, Frank Ramirez, left and came back and he had clean clothes for me. They talked, but nothing really important, just normal chatter like the hands might have over dinner. I don't even remember any of it. It wasn't important. They just stuck around the little shack for two days and then they tied my hands to the bunk and left me with the ones called Sam and José, while the other four went to keep an appointment. That's what they kept calling it, an appointment. I figured it was something nefarious, but for whatever reason, they didn't want to talk about it in front of me. They were gone a long time. The one called Sam, he and I got in an argument …" her left hand absentmindedly reached up and touched her bruised cheek, "… he ended up storming off. They returned. They hadn't been back very long when a posse arrived outside with the Sheriff of Lefors. He ordered them to drop their guns and to come out or they'd open fire he said. He gave them twenty seconds, then he started counting. There was a trapdoor and they dragged me through it and it went to the stables and the posse opened fire and they got away and there was an explosion. Then we rode most of the afternoon and I was very disoriented. I'm not really sure where we were. I know that we were near the Lazy Leaf Ranch because they said so, but I'm sure they're not there now, because they intended to not be there now. You can probably find their camp. I think I rode for about two and a half hours and they told me to ride straight South, then I'd find this place, and I did. I mean, other than everyone arguing about whose fault it was that the posse found them last night and a lot of threats on the one called Sam, because he was with the posse, there's really nothing else to tell."

Matt tapped his pencil on his notebook several times as he considered the story he had just heard. He figured as far as facts were concerned it was probably an accurate account; however, he also figured she had left out something, if not several things. He considered what he knew about this particular group of outlaws and the young woman in front of him. If he had to take a guess, he would guess that she had left out perhaps a few stolen kisses. He did not think it was anything worse than that. By all accounts, these outlaws were not out to hurt anyone. They were angry men who felt they had been robbed and cheated of their lands and wanted to get back what they thought had been stolen from them, but they were not out to hurt innocent people. In the six robberies that had been attributed to them, the only person to have been killed was the one who shot José Ramirez. He tapped his pencil again and then asked, "What did you and Sam argue about that had an outlaw fleeing and you being left behind?"

She sighed and blushed slightly. "It's really kind of ridiculous. He expressed interest in me being his wife. I told him beyond the fact that he was an outlaw, a criminal, the concept of us being married alone would be a crime. He is a colored man."

Jeffrey whistled. "Pop sure wouldn't like that."

She turned to Jeffrey and nodded. "That was what we argued about. He said that he wasn't good enough because he was a black man. I said that it was against the law. He said that my daddy wouldn't like it. I told him that Uncle Carlos and Uncle Leopold probably wouldn't like it either. It's just the world we live in." She reached up and tentatively touched her cheek. It felt very tender. "At the risk of sounding a little vain, is my face very badly bruised?"

Jeffrey reached over and tentatively touched her cheek. "Just a little, probably wouldn't show if you weren't so pale. You've been in the city too long."

She smiled, let go of Joey's hand, and hugged Jeffrey tightly. "That we can agree on completely. I've been stuck indoors too long. I'm so glad to be home."

Matt waited for them to be done embracing, then he asked, "As of yet, no one but you has ever seen their faces. Do you think you could describe them to someone so we can get some sketches of them?"

Joey started laughing. "She can probably do you one better than that. She does great little portraits. She's always been a talented artist."

She nodded. "Yes, if my luggage is here, I should have my sketchbook and pencils, everything I require. I could probably have you some drawings in an hour or two."

Joey got to his feet and shook his head. "No, not that quickly. We got you a room and I'm ordering you to take a bath and relax. You can get cleaned up, rest a little, and then at your leisure you can draw those sketches. After you've had a chance to bathe and change, you can decide whether you want to ride home, or whether you want to wait for the train tomorrow morning."

Claudette was shaking her head frantically. "No, thank you. I think I've had enough trains for a while. I think I would prefer to ride home if you gentlemen wouldn't consider that an imposition. I know it will be a long ride and we could make it in an hour or two on the train, but ..."

Joey cut her off. "Then I think it's best if we leave at first light tomorrow morning and you'll be home before supper tomorrow."

She smiled and nodded, got to her feet, and went upstairs and enjoyed a leisurely bath.

Joey waited for her to be gone before he asked Matt, "You don't believe her, do you?"

"I believe that she did not lie to us, but I do believe she's leaving stuff out. My instinct tells me what she's leaving out would be somewhat damaging to her reputation, but I don't think it is anything worse than stolen kisses. This group of men are not cold blooded criminals. Everything they do is for a purpose. Hurting her did not serve their purpose, and I believe her when she says that the others were not happy that Sam hurt her."

Joey and JR looked relieved. Jeffrey looked skeptical but chose not to comment.

Claudette greatly enjoyed her bath, and as soon as she was dry, she put on her nightgown. She would get dressed for dinner later, but for now she wanted to enjoy the freedom of not being in a corset and maybe even have a lie down, but there was something she had to do first. She seated herself at the dressing table, sketchbook in front of her, pencil in hand. She had no hesitation when it came to drawing Sam, Kenney, and Walt. She hesitated only a moment over Frank. She felt sorry for him. He did not seem like a bad guy even though she had seen him kill a man, but what he was doing was wrong and he had to be stopped. She hesitated a moment before tackling the next one. She decided on José. When she was done, she examined her drawing of José, she bit her lip, nodded, and with a heavy heart, drew Jake.

X

Texas Panhandle
Saturday, July 7, 1906

Walt rode into camp. He jumped off his horse and charged over to Frank, pulling something out of his pocket, saying with irritation as he did so, "I knew takin' that girl was gonna be the death of us. You should notta just let her go."

Frank took the offered paper, unfolded it, and read. 'WANTED $$$ 1,000 $$$ REWARD FOR THE CAPTURE OF FRANKLIN RAMIREZ BETTER KNOWN AS FRANK ROBBERY AND MURDER KNOWN ASSOCIATES JOSÉ RAMIREZ KENNETH ADAMS WALTER SHEPHERD SAMUEL GRISSOM JAKE BANKS.' Realizing there were two, he flipped to the next one. 'WANTED $$$ 500 $$$ REWARD FOR THE CAPTURE OF KENNETH ADAMS BETTER KNOWN AS KENNY ROBBERY KNOWN ASSOCIATES FRANKLIN RAMIREZ JOSÉ RAMIREZ WALTER SHEPHERD SAMUEL GRISSOM JAKE BANKS.' Holding one in each hand, he examined the images. "Not bad likenesses. Were there any others?"

Walt shrugged his shoulders. "I wasn't sticking around to find out. Those were posted on the wall by the Dry Goods store. A lot of posters up all over the place, but given the fact that it's got all of our names on it, I'd say the chances are pretty good there's posters of all of us up."

Jake and Kenny each took a poster. Kenny crumbled up his and threw it on the ground. "Damn that little tart! What were you thinking, Frank, letting her see our faces and what were you thinking, Jake, putting her on a horse and sending her away? Should've put her in the ground!"

Frank decked Kenny. "I told you before we started all this, no unnecessary killing, and we were certainly not going to kill no girl. She did us a favor. She didn't deserve to be killed for that."

Kenny got to his feet and shoved Frank. "No, she did you and José a favor. Now all of our necks are on the line. I ain't gonna swing for your crimes. I didn't kill nobody."

Jake stepped in and shoved the two of them apart. "Then you should be glad we didn't kill her. Clearly Frank is the only one wanted for murder, that means the rest of us would only do some jail time."

Walt said quickly, "I'm with Jake. I think the rest of us are in the clear for the murder, but I think we need to divide up the loot and part ways here."

"No! Hell no! We still have one more score and that's the final one. That's the big one!" snapped Frank.

Kenny was waving his hands back and forth. "No way! Forget about it! The heat is gonna be too hot! We already got one posse after us, maybe more, and now they all know what we look like. We ain't gonna be able to just stroll into town."

Frank started laughing. "Well, you see boys, that's the beauty of my plan. We ain't gotta go into town for the last score. They gonna bring it practically to us. We robbed three of their banks. We robbed two trains. They are gonna think they are bein' smart and they're gonna bring that money in by special stagecoach. That's where we're gonna get them."

Jake shook his head. "No way. I'm out. The only way we're gonna take down a special stagecoach is by killing everybody. They're too heavily armed. They'll have at least four outriders, two in front, two in back, not to mention the shotgun and anybody else they put inside as plants. That's way too many corpses."

Frank laughed again. "Not to worry, I got it all figured out. We'll wait till the stagecoach is going through that heavy rocky area where they have to slow down a little, then José and I will take out the two front outriders with bows and arrows that have been dipped in a tranquilizer strong enough to knock out a horse. They'll be out in a few seconds. We'll take out the two front stagecoach horses with the same thing, as well as the shotgun and the driver. We should be able to take out the rear outriders, so that's six all down. Then we shoot a flaming arrow into the stagecoach and when everybody comes running out, you boys will keep them covered, and they'll throw down their weapons."

Jake really did not like this, but he did not see as he had any choice. Like it or not, he was in this to the end. He stared at the wanted poster. There was one thing really bugging the hell out of him about it. Why did it not say 'kidnapping'? He shook his head. Somebody was deliberately not drawing attention to that, and that worried him.

Walt sighed and shook his head. "You make that sound really easy, and where did you get this stuff anyways, and how do we know it's gonna work?"

Frank grinned. "I got it from a friend, and if you don't think it's gonna work, we can test it on you."

*****

Two days later, Jake lay on his stomach looking out across the rocks. He still thought this entire idea was really bad and he was quite certain it was going to result in all of their deaths, but he still did not see that he had any choice in the matter. He was caught between a rock and a hard place. He just hoped everything would go according to plan. He lay there a little while longer, watching and waiting. Finally, the stagecoach came into sight. He cursed under his breath. He counted six forward outriders and the stagecoach was kicking up so much dust, he could not see if there were more. He turned to Frank. "This is a bad idea. We need to cut our losses now. If we try to get into that, we'll all end up dead."

José sighed and shook his head. "I'm with Jake. I think we're in over our heads. We made a good try for it, but it's just not going to work. They know we're coming for them and they are ready."

Frank wavered and stared at their prey, so close he could taste it, but there were only supposed to be four guards. He was sure there had to be at least twelve, and there was not supposed to be anybody in the stagecoach. He had been lied to. Had this all been a trap, a chance to cut them out? Was that what this was? He growled and started shimmying backwards. He did not know, but he was going to find out. "Come on boys, let's get out of here. This is too hot."

They were all mounted up and on their way before the stagecoach passed safely through their little trap. Frank spurred his horse and took off. After nearly an hour, Kenny demanded, "Where are we going?"

Frank replied with irritation, "We're going to ask our employer some questions."

Walt said with surprise, "I didn't know we had an employer."

Frank replied, "You think we're the only ones the Gunderson Bank's been robbing blind for years?"

It was nearing suppertime before Jake realized that they were on the Thorne ranch. He demanded, "Wait a minute, this is Howard Thorne's place! Are you telling me this whole time we been working for Howard Thorne?"

"So what if we have?" replied Frank.

Jake felt his temper rise and thought for sure he saw red. He took several deep breaths trying to calm down.

Kenny asked, "What's your problem with this Thorne fella?"

"Howard Thorne, the dirty rat bastard that he is, bought my daddy's ranch for pennies on the dollar for the overdue taxes. He's as dirty as they come. He makes bank robbers look honest. Just like him to use someone else to do his dirty work. Let them get their hands dirty while he rakes in the profits. If there's ever been a man I'd want to shoot in cold blood, it's Howard Thorne. That's why you said we had to stick around this area, and that's why you've been going after Gunderson bank."

Frank cut him off. "And what the hell is that supposed to mean?"

"Because, you stupid dumb bastard, he's been playing us all! That was where you've been disappearing off to, to get orders from him. He wanted to keep you under his thumb, and I'll bet you now that they all know our faces, he's gonna kill us all! He's a double crossing, no good, bushwhacking bastard!"

"But what has Gunderson bank have to do with any of this?" demanded Walt.

"Because, you stupid bastard, he owns it!"

Frank was shaking his head in confusion as he said, "No, James Gunderson owns the bank."

"Jesus Christ, Frankie, you got shit for brains! James Gunderson has been dead for twenty years! He's Thorne's Mama's Daddy!"

By the time they arrived at the ranch house, Frank's temper was practically burning out of control. He barely came to a stop before he leaped off his horse and charged up the front steps. José and Walt were hot on his heels, Kenny a little behind, and Jake bringing up the rear, surveying the area. It was way too quiet in his opinion. Frank slammed open the door and stormed in as he hollered, "Thorne, where are you?"

They found Thorne sitting behind his desk, a shotgun leveled at the door, two pistols and two rifles ready to hand. Thorne said with great amusement, "Pity you boys couldn't have just gotten yourselves killed like I planned on. Guess now I'm gonna have to take care of things the old-fashioned way. I mean, really, what's a ranch owner to do when five desperate men burst in on him, leaving him no choice but to take them out."

Frank snapped back, "You won't get us all, Thorne."

"I believe I have the advantage."

Jake replied with a grin. "You haven't had the advantage for weeks, not since I joined your little band."

Thorne shifted his gaze and asked, "And who exactly are you? You look familiar."

"Jake Baxter, Albert Baxter's boy."

Thorne nodded. "Oh yes, the Baxter boy who couldn't cut it ranching and left his daddy to run the place all by his self, which he couldn't do, and then your daddy got all pissed off when I bought it. He drank himself to death and now you blame me. You were a disgrace to your father, and now you think you can intimidate me."

Jake started laughing. "My daddy was a gunman who earned his living killing men. He was never cut out to be a rancher. When he met my Mama and fell in love with her, he gave her his word he would never shoot another man again, and that's the only reason you're still alive. You want to know how I became a disgrace to my Daddy? That's easy, I joined the Texas Rangers and if you don't put that shotgun down real easy like, I'm gonna really enjoy killing you."

Thorne swallowed hard. "There's only one of you, boy, and there's five of us. You think you can take us all?"

"You're right, the odds are unfair because there is one of me and only five of you, because I'm pretty sure José here, he ain't gonna give me no trouble. Kenny, well, he ain't gonna give me any trouble right now either, because he's got my knife in his ribs. Walt, well, he knows he's a lot slower than I am, and Frank, Frank might just have to die. I don't want it that way, but he might push me. And you, you ain't even got a chance because Frank's between you and me. I'll get him and then I'll put a bullet in your head. So why don't you save us all a bunch of grief and put down that shotgun and come out with your hands up."

Walt said a little unsteadily, "And what if I don't like that plan?"

"Quite frankly, Walt, you're not my priority. The Rangers sent me here to find the man with the plan. They knew Frank wasn't the one runnin' the show. They figured he was nothing more than a puppet on a string. They want the man in charge. So you see, Walt, if you don't go gettin' in my way, you can probably run out that door. I ain't gonna stop you right now because Thorne is my target."

Kenny said softly, "You ain't gotta worry about me, Jake. I ain't gonna get in your way."

Walt hesitated only a moment, then he jumped back, turned, and ran for the door. As soon as Walt started moving, Frank pushed José back. Jake also jumped to the side, out of the doorway, pulling Kenny with him. The shotgun went off. Frank hit the floor and slid a little, then started scrambling. He grabbed his side and yelled, "Jake, get that rat bastard!" He then stared in amazement as Jake took another step away from the door, lowered his pistol, and put three rounds through the wall. He shifted his gaze looking for Kenny, who was on the floor scrambling for the front door, holding his side. Clearly, he had caught some of the buckshot too.

*****

Matt and four men arrived outside the ranch house right after the five outlaws. They were just climbing the steps when they heard a shotgun go off. A moment later, three pistol rounds, then a man tried to run past them. One of the Pinkertons tackled him, taking him to the ground. Then there were three more shots. Matt drew his gun and said softly to his men, "Keep down. We don't know how many civilians are in here. So don't shoot unless shot at."

He entered carefully, peeking around the corner into the parlor. He saw three men on the floor scrambling towards him. One man was on his feet reloading a gun.

Matt yelled out, "Pinkerton National Detective Agency! Throw down your guns or we'll open fire!"

In response, someone in the office fired several shots in their direction. The man who had just finished reloading his gun aimed for the wall and pulled the trigger three times, then he shifted towards the office door, shouting as he did so, "You don't have a chance, Thorne! You can't go up against a Ranger and the Pinkertons! You got nowhere to run and nowhere to hide!"

There was a long moment's silence, then Jake heard gurgling. He dropped down a little lower and peeked through the doorway. Through the hole under the desk, he could see Thorne slumped in the chair, his hand groping for the rifle, blood running out of his mouth. He got up and moved in, quickly grabbing the rifle off the floor.

Matt followed the young man in a little warily. He pulled all of the guns on the desk away from the man in the chair. Thorne gasped out. "Only Frank

would be stupid enough to join up with a Ranger."
His body shuddered, and then he died.

Jake stared at the Pinkerton. After a moment, he reached into his pocket and pulled out his wallet, opened it, and retrieved his badge from where he had concealed it. Pinning it on his chest, he said, "Jake Baxter, Texas Ranger. Where on earth did the Pinkertons come from?" He finished pinning on his badge and extended his hand to the Pinkerton.

Matt took his hand and shook it. "Matt Crawford, Pinkerton's National Detective Agency. We were hired by Mr. and Mrs. McLoughlin to retrieve their daughter, Claudette McLoughlin."

Jake, who was moving around the desk, looked over his shoulder quickly in surprise, inadvertently changing directions and slamming into the side of the desk. He murmured, "Ow, dammit!" After a moment he reminded himself, *Keep your mind on the job at hand, forget about her,* and continued on around the desk and pulled the body out of the chair, saying as he did so, "Nice to meet you, Mr. Crawford." He hesitated a long moment then added, "I hope Miss McLoughlin made it safely to town?"

Matt looked the younger man up and down, then reached into his coat pocket and handed over a stack of papers, saying as he did so, "It takes a hell of a lot of nerve to go up against these guys by yourself."

Jake grinned and replied, "Well, you know what they say. 'One riot, one Ranger.'"

Matt chuckled. "And I seem to recall Bill saying he was constantly misquoted on that."

Jake shrugged his shoulders and laughed. "I know, but it sounds real good. And at least for once, if the damn reporters are gonna misquote you, they made you sound better rather than worse." He took the offered papers with his left hand.

Matt laughed, then said, "True enough." He made a circular motion with his hand encompassing the area. "Now, about this mess. Would you like the Pinkertons to clean it up for you, or would you prefer to handle it?" He shifted his gaze to the body. He dropped down on one knee to examine it closer, then he looked over his shoulder and demanded, "How many shots were fired at him?"

"I fired at him nine times, and as far as the situation is concerned, I think I have it well in hand, thank you." He pointed his gun at Frank. "Be a real pity, Frank, if you make me shoot you. That goes for you too, Kenny. I can hear you crawling away. It ain't like you're gonna get too far anyways. I'm pretty sure this ain't the only Pinkerton here." He decided he did not have time to look at these papers right this minute. He stuck them in his pocket and went and tied up Frank, Kenny, and José. While he was tying up José, he asked, "Out of curiosity, why ask how many times I shot at him?"

"Intellectual curiosity. After all, it appeared as though you were shooting at him through the wall, and he's got eight rounds in him."

Jake frowned. "Dammit, that means I missed once. Tough old bastard. Who'd of thought he'd been able to take eight rounds." He went to retrieve his prisoner from the Pinkertons.

XI

Lazy Leaf Ranch, Texas
Wednesday, July 11, 1906

Dani sat crocheting, discreetly watching her daughter struggle to focus on her needlepoint. Dani was very worried about her daughter. Caleb was practically beside himself with worry. She seemed unusually quiet these past few days. Dani had reminded herself and Caleb on several occasions that they did not know whether this was unusually quiet or not. They had only seen Claudette over the holidays. Dani thought that she seemed quieter then, not at all like the child who had left for school, but Caleb was convinced that something horrible had happened to his child and she was too afraid or ashamed to tell them. Dani did not think that was the case at all. She did think that something had happened that Claudette was not talking about, but her motherly instincts were telling her it was something different. They were interrupted by Caleb entering. He spoke as he hung his hat up. "Well, we can all rest easy now. They caught all those outlaws. One of them was apprehended in Amarillo trying to board a train, the one called Sam. That was three days ago. The others were all apprehended two days ago."

Claudette shot to her feet and asked, "How did you hear this?"

He held up several papers. "It was in the Pampa paper yesterday. Our newspaper picked up the articles and ran it today, but I have both papers."

She crossed to her father and held out her hand. "May I read them?"

Caleb frowned, reached out, and caressed his daughter's cheek. To his horror, she blushed slightly and looked away. "Claudette, my love, I really don't think that's a good idea. I think you need to put this whole thing behind you, and I think we all need to stop talking about it now that we all know that they've been apprehended."

She interrupted him. "Please, Father, I'd like to read the articles for myself. I'm not a child."

Caleb frowned and glanced at his wife. She nodded. He grudgingly handed the papers over. To his further astonishment, his daughter took them, hesitated only a moment, then hurried upstairs to her bedroom. He watched her go, then turned back to his wife. "What the devil is that all about?"

Dani smiled, then she sighed and frowned. She got up and crossed to her husband, wrapping her arms around his waist. "I'm starting to think our little girl might have a very big girl attraction to one of those outlaws."

Caleb gripped his wife by the shoulders and pushed her to arms reach. "Oh, hell no! Don't even joke about that! That's not even funny! I'll not have my daughter ..."

Dani cut him off. "Lower your voice. You don't want her to hear you."

"I don't give a damn if she does. I will not have my daughter in love with a common criminal!"

Dani smiled up at him mischievously. "And who says he's common? Maybe he's very good looking."

"Dani, don't be ridiculous! This is not a laughing matter. Would you have your daughter marry an outlaw ... You don't think our daughter made a very foolish mistake with one of those outlaws, do you?"

"I would like to think I raised my daughter better than that, but we're all human and we all ... make mistakes." She looked at him meaningfully.

"You have got to find out, because if one of those pigs laid one finger on my little girl, I'll make sure they never find the body."

"Caleb, I cannot force our daughter to confide in me, and what makes you so worried all of a sudden?"

"When I rubbed her cheek just now, she got all embarrassed. She never used to do that."

*****

Claudette closed and bolted the door behind her. She hurried over to her dressing table and began pouring over the papers. It did not mention any of the outlaws by name, but it did mention that one was killed and two were wounded during their apprehension. The paper also said that the trial of the survivors was going to take place today. She frowned and read them again. She thought that it was very odd, usually papers listed all of their names, or at least they did in New York. She did not remember reading papers before she moved to New York. Maybe things were just different in Texas. She sighed and told herself firmly, *It doesn't matter how nice they were. They were all outlaws who robbed people, hurt people. You should not be praying for mercy for them, but justice.*

Claudette spent the next two days waiting for someone to go to town and come back with more papers. Her parents had become even more overprotective. She had thought they would let up now that the outlaws had been apprehended, but they seem to have gotten even worse. She desperately wanted to ride into town herself and get the papers, but she was afraid if she said that, her father would have kittens, so she decided it was best to just wait. Sooner or later, one of the hands would go into town to get the mail and the newspapers. The post office held them with their mail. The waiting and not knowing was just killing her. She did not like thinking of Frank being hanged. She might have wanted to shoot him herself, but she did not think he deserved to be hanged. The man on the train had not exactly been innocent. *Oh, for the love of God, what is wrong with me?* She squirmed in her chair, then she decided she could not stand it any longer. She got to her feet and threw her embroidery in the basket. She charged upstairs and changed into her riding clothes. She stood in her bedroom a long moment, contemplating what she was about to do. She had done it a few times when she was a child and her father had never caught her, but here she was, eighteen years old and about to climb out the window because she felt like her parents were smothering her. But she knew if she went downstairs and said she wanted to go riding, her father would tell her it was not a good day, just like he had done yesterday. She was on the verge of shooting him. "Lord, forgive me for what I'm about to do," she said aloud as she quietly opened the window and judged the distance from the window to the tree. She grabbed her boots off the bed and carefully dropped them out the window, then she climbed onto the window, reached up, and grabbed a large tree branch. She dangled for only a moment before she was able to pull up her legs up, swing one over the branch, and then start climbing down the tree. She murmured to herself, "You know, Claudette, this is very unladylike and Miss Josephine would be appalled." She considered that for a moment, and then she murmured, "Well, Miss Josephine can go hang. She's never been locked in her house before." Reaching the ground, she picked up her boots, dusted off her feet and slipped them on, then hurried to the stable, hoping desperately that her father had not left any hands in the stables. To her relief, when she entered, they were empty. She grabbed her saddle and was halfway to a stall when she heard someone behind her. She jumped and turned quickly.

Leopold stood there with his arms crossed over his chest. When he locked eyes with her, he demanded, "Does your daddy know what you're up to?"

She stood there looking stricken for a long moment. "No."

Leopold crossed to her and took the saddle from her. "Back inside with you."

"Oh, please, Uncle Leopold, I just want to go for a ride. I am tired of being cooped up in that house."

Leopold sighed, reached out, and patted her on the shoulder. "I know, Sweetie, but you have to understand your parents are gonna be a little overprotective for a while. Why don't you ask your daddy to take you riding?"

She sighed. "I tried that yesterday and he said it wasn't a good day. Something tells me today is not gonna be any better. I wish I knew what was wrong with them. I don't remember them being like this when I was ten."

Leopold returned the saddle, then turned to face her. "It might have something to do with the fact that they think you're lying to them. You ain't never been good at lying and everyone thinks you're hidin' something. Maybe if you told them what you don't want them to know, everybody can get back to normal because I'm gonna tell you right now, girl, your daddy ain't bearable to work with right now."

She frowned as she considered that. "If I tell my daddy that two of the outlaws kissed me, do you think he'll ever let me out his sight again?"

Leopold asked a little nervously, "Is that all they did?"

"Yes, of course, don't be ridiculous. Frank may have been an outlaw, but he wasn't evil. And as far as Sam is concerned, I think if he tried any more, José would've shot him."

He gave a little nervous laugh as he said, "Claudette, young lady, if you tell your daddy that two of those outlaws kissed you, he will be so relieved. I promise you things around here will settle down."

She frowned. She was not sure she believed that, but Uncle Leopold had never led her wrong before, she did not think he would start now. "Very well, but if I get grounded for the rest of my life, I'm blaming you."

He roared with laughter. "If you get grounded for the rest your life, I'll bring a horse out to your window at midnight." Claudette started laughing and hugged him tightly. "Now go on and get in the house, have a conversation with your parents. Then things can get back to normal around here before I shoot Caleb."

Claudette practically ran back to the house. She was in such a hurry to get this over and done with, she burst through the front door without even looking and slammed into someone. She looked up expecting it to be one of the hands. He turned around, opening his mouth to speak. Her eyes widened and she said without thinking, "Jake, what in God's name are you doing here?"

Jake hesitated, then said somewhat nervously, "My apologies, ma'am, you all right?"

Dani watched her daughter's cheeks take on the faintest pink hue. She gripped her husband by the arm and pulled him back towards one of the dining room tables. Caleb looked at her and opened his mouth to speak. She put a finger to her lips and pointed for them to watch. Caleb made a face, shrugged his shoulders, crossed his arms over his chest, perched on the edge of the table and stretched out his legs, crossing them at the ankles.
Apparently there was going to be a show, or at least his wife thought so.

Claudette stared at Jake for a long moment, then asked, "Care to explain exactly what you're apologizing for, and why are you here?" As she was speaking, her eyes flicked over him. His blonde hair had been cut so now he looked quite respectable and he was clean shaven. He was wearing a dark blue cavalry bib shirt, which really brought out the blue of his eyes. Her eyes widened when she saw a Texas Ranger badge pinned on his chest. She pointed at it and stared for a moment, then looked up at him. He opened his mouth but did not get a chance to speak because she slapped him across the face.

Caleb started to stand up. Dani put her hand on his hip, pressing him back against the table. He shrugged his shoulders and crossed his arms again. Clearly his wife knew something he did not.

Jake cleared his throat. "I might have deserved that." In response, Claudette slapped him again. She pulled back her hand to slap him a third time. This time, he caught her wrist. "I'm pretty sure I deserved the first one. I might have even deserved the second one. Care to explain why I deserve to be slapped a third time?"

"Really? You have to even ask? I think I could slap you a hundred times and it would be justified!"

"Now wait a minute, what did I ever do to you? I was nice to you."

Claudette stomped her foot, balled up her fists at her side and growled, "Really? Nice to me? Nice to me?" She held out her left hand and began ticking off on her fingers as she spoke. "You forced me to drink whiskey. You looked at me while I was bathing, God only knows how many times. You tied me to the bunk and left me alone with Sam. You nearly got me killed by a posse. You threw me over a horse. I think at some point and time you made me drink more whiskey, and we won't even talk about the last night ..."

Caleb and Dani exchanged looks.

"... And now I learn that you're a Texas Ranger!"

Jake cleared his throat and nodded somberly. "Yes, ma'am, I did most of that."

She stomped her foot again. "Most of it?"

"Yes, ma'am, most of it, because I still maintain that posse was just as likely to kill you as they were us."

She growled. "Very well, I will grant you that one. Now, Mr. Texas Ranger, care to explain what you're doing here?" He opened his mouth to speak, but she cut him off. "Is Jake even your real name?"

"Yes, ma'am, Jake Baxter."

"Will you please stop calling me ma'am, or have you forgotten my name? Not that any of you ever used it, you seemed to find 'girl' or 'Missy' sufficient."

"I remember your name just fine, ma'am, but I think it's more proper under the circumstances if I call you ma'am, unless you prefer Miss McLoughlin."

She crossed her arms over her chest and said coldly, "And exactly what circumstances are we talking about?"

"Amongst the things that the outlaws had stolen, we have recovered some personal items that we have identified their owners, and I'm here to return your reticule, ma'am."

Claudette looked even more irritated. "Let me see if I understand you correctly. The only reason you're here is to return my reticule?"

He nodded. "Yes, ma'am."

Claudette clasped her hands tightly in front of her. She nodded several times to herself. "Of course, that makes perfect sense. I guess you can give it to me and you can be on your way."

He cleared his throat. "Actually, Miss McLoughlin, I have already given it to your folks."

She suddenly remembered. "By the way, your saddle is in the stables – unless, of course, you stole it. In that case, you can tell us who the owner is and we'll return it to them: but when we returned the horse to its owner, he said that he'd only lost the horse, not a saddle, and wouldn't take it. So Father put it in the stables, in case the owner showed up."

"Yes, ma'am, that's my saddle. I'll be sure to take it with me when I leave. Thank you for holding onto it, but come to think of it, I might just have one little question if you have a moment."

"If there's anything I can do to help the Texas Rangers, I would be glad to be of service to the Texas Rangers. What can I clear up for the Texas Rangers?"

Jake wondered if she could manage to squeeze Texas Rangers in that sentence any more times. He unbuttoned one of the buttons in his shirt and pulled out a few pieces of paper. He unfolded them and showed her the one on top. "It was about this. You see, when I first saw it, I thought somewhere between the artist and the printing press something must a happened, but Mr. Crawford was real helpful and gave me the original sketches."

Claudette barely glanced at the sketches in his hand. She did not bother to take them. She knew what they looked like, after all, she had drawn them. "What about them?"

"Why was everyone else's accurate but José's and mine?"

Caleb looked at his wife and raised an eyebrow. She shrugged her shoulders.

She looked down at the floor. "Are the Texas Rangers going to charge me with impeding an investigation, or whatever you call it, interference?"

"Nobody knows but Crawford and me. Why?"

"Because José is sixteen years old. He was just following his older brother, a man he idolizes. I figured he deserves a chance. Figured maybe if he got shy of Frank, he'd settle down and be honest. You never acted like much of a criminal. If you are going to charge me, charge me. Otherwise, are we done?" She sniffed, fighting back tears.

Jake hesitated a long moment, then he pitched his voice low. "Look, ma'am, the life of a Texas Ranger is hard. You never know whether you're going to come home or not. You learn pretty quick better not to have anything that relies on you. You see too many of your fellow Rangers put in the dirt. Too many wailing widows …"

Caleb put his hand over his face, leaned over, and whispered softly, "Please tell me I did not sound that stupid."

Dani smiled and patted him on the shoulder and whispered back. "Oh no, my dear, you sounded much stupider."

"... better not have anything tied to you." When he finished speaking, Jake hesitated a moment, then he picked up his hat, nodded to her, put it on his head, and walked out.

"Want I should shoot him in the leg?" questioned Caleb.

"No, thank you, Daddy, that's completely unnecessary."

Dani nudged her husband and jerked her head in the direction of the door. He nodded, got up and headed for the door, trying to figure out what he was supposed to say, but he knew one thing for sure, he sure as hell was not going to ask about 'the last night'. He knew exactly what went through the mind of a young man when dealing with a pretty girl. He did not need to hear any of that in regards to his own daughter. As he walked down the steps, he was not exactly surprised to see the young man staring at his horse. Walking behind him, Caleb murmured, "That was a nice load of bullshit."

Jake turned around. "Excuse me, sir?"

"I'm just saying that that was a bunch of bullshit. If you're not interested in my daughter, you should just say you're not interested, or you shouldn't even bring the subject up. But giving her some line about being a Texas Ranger is a dangerous job, that's a load a shit."

"What? You think the life of a Texas Ranger isn't dangerous?"

"No, I think you're using that as an excuse." Caleb turned around and gestured. "Over there a couple hours ride used to be the Patterson place. It's mine now. Paul Patterson was a good man, hard working, and he fought like hell to keep that ranch. It's just a little spread, but it was his. One day he didn't come home. Next morning his wife and son went looking for him. Found him in the bottom of a gully wash, him and his horse, both dead. We never figured out whether the horse got spooked and that was what sent them tumbling down the wash, or whether Patterson was just in a hurry to get home and it was after dark. Either way doesn't really matter, he's dead. His wife decided there was just no way with three small children she could keep the place. Now she lives in town. I grew up on this ranch. My blood is in the soil in more than a few places. I've been shot on this ranch four times, twice almost killed me. I'm just a rancher. Patterson ran the assayer's office and was just a rancher. Now, I repeat, you're just using that bunch of bullshit to protect yourself from getting hurt. Trust me on this kiddo, I've been there. Any one of us could die, any day, any time."

"So you tell me this, honestly. You wouldn't rather your daughter marry some nice quiet rancher compared to a Texas Ranger? When ranchers get shot at, it's unusual. My job is getting shot at. My job is taking on five outlaws by myself. If I die, where's that leave your daughter?"

"What I would rather really doesn't matter. What matters is who she loves, and I'm starting to think my wife has been right this whole time and that her problem is she fell in love with one of you idiots. Though I'm starting to think one of the outlaws might be smarter than the Ranger who brought them in. And if you think my Claudette can't take care of herself, you don't know her at all."

Jake cleared his throat. He hesitated a long moment, then asked, "Mr. McLoughlin, may I have your permission to call on your daughter?"

"It's late. Why don't you stay for dinner and bunk in the bunkhouse, and we'll have that conversation in the morning."

The End